As they passed the front desk the maître d' bowed slightly. *"Bonsoir,"* he said.

"Bonsoir," Lila responded, taking a box of matches from the bowl on the stand. Steven's eyes widened, and he looked at her for an explanation. But she just casually tucked the matches in her purse and pushed open the door. Steven followed her out of the restaurant, feeling worried again.

"What are the matches for?" Steven asked casually as they walked across the lot.

"Oh, it's just a little souvenir," Lila responded lightly. "I always take matches from restaurants."

Steven absorbed the information with alarm. Lila loved candlelight, and she collected matches. He thought of her expression as she had lit the candles in the restaurant. She had looked almost hypnotized. *Is she a pyromaniac?* Steven wondered. *Is she playing with me? Is this some kind of cat-and-mouse game?*

Lila turned and gave him a bright smile, a smile that was just for him. Steven's pulse picked up at her affectionate gaze. And the note of danger just made his heart beat faster.

Visit the Official Sweet Valley Web Site on the Internet at:

http://www.sweetvalley.com

LILA'S
NEW FLAME

Written by
Kate William

Created by
FRANCINE PASCAL

BANTAM BOOKS
NEW YORK · TORONTO · LONDON · SYDNEY · AUCKLAND

RL 6, age 12 and up

LILA'S NEW FLAME
A Bantam Book / November 1997

Sweet Valley High® is a registered trademark of Francine Pascal.
Conceived by Francine Pascal.
Produced by Daniel Weiss Associates, Inc.
33 West 17th Street
New York, NY 10011.
Cover photography by Michael Segal.

ISBN: 0-553-57069-2

Published simultaneously in the United States and Canada

Bantam Books are published by Bantam Books, a division of Bantam
Doubleday Dell Publishing Group, Inc. Its trademark, consisting of the
words "Bantam Books" and the portrayal of a rooster, is Registered in U.S.
Patent and Trademark Office and in other countries. Marca Registrada.
Bantam Books, 1540 Broadway, New York, New York 10036.

PRINTED IN THE UNITED STATES OF AMERICA

OPM   0 9 8 7 6 5 4 3 2 1

To Anita Lora Kaller

Chapter 1

Sixteen-year-old Lila Fowler sat cross-legged on her four-poster canopy bed on Friday night, a gold-framed picture in her hand. A handsome face with warm brown eyes smiled out at her from the photo. Lila gazed sadly at the familiar image, feeling like her heart was breaking in two.

"Good-bye, Bo," Lila whispered aloud. Bo had called her the night before to break up. *I was just calling to say hello,* he had said. But actually he had been calling to say good-bye. Forever.

Lila pulled her knees up to her chest, her heart heavy. She couldn't believe it was really over. It seemed like it had just begun.

She could still remember the balmy sunny day when she had first caught sight of Bo. Their eyes had locked, and her heartbeat had accelerated. Lila had known immediately that he was the one for her.

Lila and Bo had met while they were junior counselors at Camp Echo Mountain, a performing arts camp in the mountains of Montana. Bo was a cute guy with curly brown hair and a crooked smile. At first he had given Lila the impression that he was a real back-to-nature type who loved mountain biking and rock climbing. So Lila had pretended to be just like him. She had started dressing in khaki shorts and cotton T-shirts and had become an expert in herbs and nature teas.

But then one night Bo had confessed. He admitted that his name was actually Beauregard Creighton the Third and that he came from a wealthy family in Washington, D.C. He had just been trying to impress Lila with his mountain man act. When the truth came out and they discovered that they really were alike, Lila had felt that she had met her soul mate. The first thing she and Bo had done was order a gourmet meal sent Express Mail to camp from Sweet Valley. Lila laughed softly at the memory, feeling a bittersweet pang in her heart.

After that, Lila and Bo had been inseparable. It turned out they had everything in common. They shared a love for travel and a taste for the finer things in life. Lila's mother had spent years living in France, and Bo's mother went to the Paris fashion shows twice a year. Lila and Bo had spent much of their time at camp walking along the beautiful lakefront, discussing their travel adventures and reciting French poetry.

At the end of the summer they had vowed to stay together. And they had been successful for a while. They had kept up an active correspondence, and they had even met up once in New York City. But eventually their letters and phone calls had slowed down. Both of their lives started changing, and the gap between them grew wider and wider.

Lila could still hear Bo's uncomfortable voice on the phone the night before. "Lila, I think we need to talk," he had said. The pain in his voice had matched the pain in her heart.

Lila sighed. She knew it was for the best. It was impossible to keep up a long-distance relationship, and she and Bo had ended on good terms. But still, Lila couldn't help feeling miserable. It had been nice to know Bo was in her life, to anticipate his phone calls and romantic letters. Now she felt like she was all alone in the world.

And I really am *alone,* Lila thought, feeling sorry for herself. She slid off her bed and wrapped her arms around herself, listening to the silence. The house was completely deserted. Her parents were vacationing on a remote island somewhere in the South Pacific and couldn't even be reached by phone. The butler had the weekend off, and Lucinda, the maid, had left for the evening.

Fresh tears came to Lila's eyes and spilled down her cheeks. Lila crossed the rug and grabbed a tissue out of the box on her bureau, wiping away her tears. She glanced around her room, taking in the antique furniture, the ornate mirrors, the walk-in closets, then pulled open one of the closet doors and studied the fashionable skirts and dresses hanging up in long, neat rows. *All this,* she thought. *For what? A Friday night home alone.*

Feeling disgusted, Lila yanked open her bedroom door and headed down the hall. Her soft red skirt swished lightly around her ankles. As she descended the long, winding staircase the house echoed strangely. The mansion seemed huge and hollow. Feeling chilled in her thin cotton skirt and white T-shirt, she wrapped her arms tightly around her chest.

For once Lila noticed the grandeur of Fowler Crest. The huge, twenty-room Spanish-style mansion was replete with a fountain, an Olympic-size swimming pool, and luxurious, sculptured grounds. But normally Lila wasn't aware of the splendor of the estate. Usually it just seemed like home. Now she felt like she was living in some sort of museum.

Lila walked into the living room, which her mother had recently redecorated to resemble a French salon. Mint green velvet divans sat in the middle of the floor, and gilded eighteenth-century portraits hung on the walls. Two beautiful white marble statues stood in the corner. Lila scowled. This wasn't a living room. It was a showplace. It was meant for displaying works of art, not for living in.

She crossed the floor quickly and headed into the dining room. A long rectangular glass table

4

stretched the length of the room, and two solid oak breakfronts holding imported liqueurs and fine china stood against the wall. This was where her parents entertained. This was where they held parties for ambassadors and celebrities and important people in the business world. And this was where Lila had eaten her dinner all alone this evening.

Lila pushed through the glass French doors leading into the ballroom. An imposing black grand piano stood in the corner, and high-backed upholstered gold chairs were scattered about the floor. The most impressive feature was the baroque painting that covered the arched ceiling, depicting a Mother Earth figure surrounded by tiny, flying angels.

Lila crossed the pink marble floor, hearing her footsteps resonate in the airy salon. She stood still in the middle of the room, feeling like a stranger in her own home.

I have all this, Lila thought dryly, spreading her arms wide. She slumped down in a velvet gold chair, a tear in her eye. *Nothing.*

"I am *so* psyched that Steven is coming home tomorrow!" Jessica Wakefield exclaimed on Friday evening. She was standing at the counter of the cheerful, yellow Wakefield kitchen, chopping up walnuts on a wooden cutting board.

"So am I," her twin sister, Elizabeth, agreed from the table, where she was outlining the letters of a big Welcome Home sign.

Jessica and Elizabeth were planning a brunch for their older brother, Steven, who was returning the next day. Steven was a freshman at Sweet Valley University. A prelaw student, Steven planned to one day become an attorney like his father. He had been given a fantastic opportunity to do an internship with the Sweet Valley District Attorney's office and would be staying at home all semester.

"It's too bad Mom and Dad aren't around," Elizabeth remarked, reaching for a felt-tipped green marker from the middle of the table. "Then we could have really had a family reunion." Their mother, an interior designer, was attending a conference in Chicago, and their father had accompanied her for the weekend.

Jessica threw a quick look over at her sister to see if she was kidding. But Elizabeth looked entirely serious as she shaded in the letters of her banner. Jessica dumped her chopped-up nuts into a bowl of muffin batter, shaking her head. Was Elizabeth crazy? It was *great* that their parents were out of town for the weekend. That meant they could do something really wild—like have a huge party.

Jessica stirred her batter, pondering the idea. With no parents to worry about for two whole days, they could have the bash of the season. In fact, they could have a surprise party and invite all Steven's friends as well. And since it would be a

6

surprise, Steven couldn't possibly refuse. Jessica smiled to herself. Sometimes she even impressed herself with her brilliance.

"I think we should throw a big bash tomorrow night to welcome Steven back," Jessica announced. "We could invite everyone and have a live band, like the Droids." The more she thought about it, the more Jessica was getting excited about the idea.

"Whoa!" Elizabeth said, holding up a hand. "I don't think Mom and Dad would be too thrilled about the idea of us having a party when they're not around." She cocked her head and studied her work. Then she picked up a fuchsia marker and began coloring in a letter.

Jessica rolled her eyes. "That's exactly the point, dummy. Since they're not here, they don't have to know." She leaned over to preheat the oven.

"Jess, do you remember what happened the last time we threw a party without permission?" Elizabeth pointed out.

Jessica's lips turned down in a scowl as she thought back to the event. Not so long ago she and Elizabeth had visited Steven at Sweet Valley University. He had gone away with his girlfriend for the weekend, and Jessica had grabbed hold of the opportunity to transform his apartment into the social event of the season. By the time Elizabeth got wind of the idea, Jessica had already invited half the freshman class. The party had been a huge success, but unfortunately Steven had

7

walked in right in the middle of it. He had been furious.

"That was different," Jessica said finally. "Steven was mad because we had a party behind his back. This time we'll be throwing a party *for* him. He'll be thrilled." She reached up into a cabinet and pulled out an aluminum cupcake pan.

"Well, I don't think Mom and Dad will be," Elizabeth said, scraping back her chair and crossing the floor. "If you recall, they grounded us for a month after our party at SVU." Elizabeth pulled open a kitchen drawer and began rummaging around in it.

Jessica sighed. Elizabeth was clearly in her self-righteous mode. "But Steven will be here to chaperone," Jessica protested. "If Mom and Dad find out about it, I'm sure they won't mind." She tied her thick blond hair back in a knot and began carefully ladling mix into the pan. "Besides, *they're* the ones who abandoned us for the weekend. I think they just wanted an excuse to be alone. It's not fair if we don't get to enjoy the opportunity as well."

Elizabeth laughed as she headed back to the table, a big pair of scissors in her hand. "Jessica Wakefield, you will find any excuse to have a party."

Jessica sniffed, blowing a loose strand of hair out of her eyes. "It is *not* an excuse. Steven is coming home for the entire semester. This is the first time in years we'll get to spend a lot of time with him. I think that's an excellent reason."

"I think you just want to have a party," Elizabeth insisted, sitting down at the table and lifting her sign into the air.

Jessica crossed her arms over her chest. "And so what if I do? Is that a crime?"

Elizabeth grinned. "A slight misdemeanor." Holding up the banner with one hand, she began carefully cutting some excess paper from the end.

Jessica pulled open the oven door and slid the aluminum pan in. "Well, do you have a better idea for Saturday night?"

"Todd and I were thinking of hanging out and renting a video," Elizabeth said, squinting at the sign as she worked.

Jessica rolled her eyes. "Sounds like fun," she remarked. "Part two of *Boresville, the Movie: Elizabeth and Todd Rent a Video.*"

"Very cute, Jess," Elizabeth returned. Suddenly the banner slid out of her hand to the floor. "Shoot," Elizabeth muttered underneath her breath, reaching over to retrieve it.

Jessica felt like screaming. Her sister was completely unshakable this evening. "I can't believe you would rather watch a video than have a party," she persisted. She climbed up on a wooden stool and drummed her fingertips on the countertop.

"Jessica, that is not the point," Elizabeth said firmly, smoothing the sign down on the table. "I am *not* throwing a party behind Mom and Dad's backs. End of discussion."

9

Jessica scowled and slumped down on her stool. Clearly her sister wasn't going to change her mind. This weekend was going to be a total waste.

Sometimes she couldn't believe she and Elizabeth were even related. The twins were identical in appearance, from their wavy golden blond hair to their ocean blue eyes to their lovely heart-shaped faces. But the resemblances stopped at the surface. Inside, the girls were as different as night and day.

Jessica loved excitement. A cocaptain of the cheerleading squad and an active member of Sweet Valley's most exclusive sorority, Pi Beta Alpha, Jessica could always be found at the center of the action. Her favorite activities were shopping at the mall, swimming in the ocean, and dancing at the beach disco. As soon as there was a moment's calm in Sweet Valley, Jessica was sure to shake things up.

Elizabeth, on the other hand, preferred to lay low. She was a staff writer for the *Oracle,* the school newspaper, and actively involved in extracurricular activities. Elizabeth had high aspirations to be a journalist one day and spent much of her time reading novels and writing poetry. In her spare time she could usually be found hanging out with her best friends, Enid Rollins and Maria Slater, or taking a walk along the beach with her longtime boyfriend, Todd Wilkins.

Jessica hopped off her stool and paced the

Spanish-tiled floor, her mind clicking. There was no way she could let this opportunity pass. They had the whole weekend ahead of them, and Jessica was determined to use it.

Maybe Lila will have an idea, she thought, reaching for the phone on the wall to call her best friend. She could always count on Lila to be her partner in fun.

But then Jessica hesitated. Lila was going through a difficult time. She seemed to be in some kind of depression. She and Bo had just broken up last night, and she had looked miserable in school that day.

Then Jessica shrugged. It would do Lila good to get out a bit. Sitting around the house feeling sorry for herself wasn't going to make her feel any better.

Jessica picked up the phone and punched in Lila's phone number. Cradling the receiver in the crook of her neck, she tapped her foot on the floor as she waited for Lila to answer. But the phone just rang and rang.

Jessica placed the receiver on the hook slowly. *That's funny,* she said to herself. *Lila told me she wasn't going out tonight. And why didn't the machine pick up?*

Jessica stared into space, deep in thought. It wasn't a big deal that Lila wasn't home. After all, she could have run out to the store or gone for a walk. Or maybe she didn't feel like talking on the phone. But for some reason Jessica had a feeling that something else was going on.

"Hey, Jess, you want to help me out here?" Elizabeth interrupted her thoughts. Jessica looked over to find her sister standing on a chair, stringing up her sign.

"Huh? Oh, yeah," Jessica said. She climbed up on a chair next to Elizabeth and took the other side of the banner, forcing the eerie premonition out of her mind.

Seventeen-year-old Devon Whitelaw strapped his backpack firmly to the rear of his Harley-Davidson motorcycle, his face grim. He was finally getting out of this little Connecticut town. He had packed only the essentials—some clothes, his favorite books, a few letters. He was leaving everything else behind.

Devon took one last look at the imposing house where he had spent most of his youth. The white brick estate was shrouded in darkness, and a FOR SALE sign was propped up on the overgrown front lawn. In the misty night air it looked like a phantom house. And that's all it was now—the ghostly reminder of an empty past.

Devon's parents had been killed recently in a car accident. They had been driving along a main highway in Geneva on business when a car had spun out of control and crashed into them. Apparently they were killed immediately. The entire town of Westwood, Connecticut, had been shocked, as well as the New York business community. After the accident the phone had rung off the hook with calls of sympathy and support.

But Devon had remained untouched. In fact, he barely noticed his parents' absence. His father had been involved in high finance and his mother was a professional socialite. They had spent most of their time traveling, visiting clients and attending society affairs. Devon's childhood had consisted of a series of surrogate parents—nannies and maids and boarding school instructors.

Left to fend for himself, Devon had been forced to grow up fast. He had spent most of his childhood alone. Nobody had ever noticed his brilliant schoolwork or his impeccable report cards. And nobody had ever monitored his activities. Frustrated by his solitude, Devon went out almost every evening. He made his appearance at all the high-school parties in town and rode his motorcycle late into the night.

Although he was still a junior in high school, Devon looked older than his age. He was about six feet tall, with a lean and muscular frame. Even his face had the maturity of an adult's. He had a strong, square jaw, full red lips, and deep slate blue eyes with a serious expression in them.

Devon had wanted to go off on his own months ago, but his parents wouldn't give him his independence. "We're a family," his mother had said. "We have to stick together." But her words had been just that—words. She was more concerned about appearances than she was about her son's well-being. So Devon had been forced to attend high school in his small town while his parents spent their time jet-setting around the world. It was his role to keep up a semblance of normality for the benefit of his parents' clients and friends.

But now he was really and truly on his own—and Devon was ready for it. He was ready to forge a life for himself. Now that his family was gone, there was nothing to keep him here. And he planned to get as far away from this small town as possible.

Devon leaned back against the bike, taking in the quiet, staid neighborhood. He looked at the ritzy estates, the well-groomed lawns, the fancy cars. If the whole town went up in flames, Devon reflected, he wouldn't care. And with his powerful grasp of physics and chemistry it would be easy to make it happen.

For a moment he berated himself for his black thoughts. But then he shrugged. The world would be better off if places like this didn't exist. He'd had it with the gossiping and back-stabbing of small-town life. He was sick of the girls who only saw him as a chiseled face and the guys who coveted what he had.

And what did he have, really? What did he ever have? A mother who was too busy with her own emotional baggage to deal with him and a father who needed to control his family as completely as he controlled his business empire.

Even in death his father maintained his hold over Devon. His will stated that Devon had to select a suitable guardian in order to collect his inheritance and that he had to stay with that person until he reached the age of twenty-one. Once he found a guardian, Devon would receive ten million dollars, half of his inheritance. He would receive the other half when he turned twenty-one.

Devon was furious at the restraints on his life. He finally had his freedom, but he was forced to remain dependent.

Shaking his head in disgust, he slung a long leg over his motorcycle seat. There was only one solution, one cure for his anger and loneliness and frustration. He would have to find a guardian who would provide a truly caring home, the kind of home he had never had before.

Devon looked up at the North Star, which had just appeared in the dusky sky. He wanted a life with a sense of true light, he thought, a light to guide him on his way. He wanted to find something truly meaningful. And some*one* truly genuine—to ease his sense of the void.

But did that kind of perfection exist? Or was he destined for disappointment?

Devon zipped up his brown leather bomber jacket and put on his motorcycle helmet. Then he revved the engine and took off without a backward glance.

Lila sat before a crackling fire in the living room of Fowler Crest late Friday night, a stack of worn love letters in her hand. She had spent the evening rereading Bo's correspondence, and she felt like his beautiful words were engraved in her mind.

She unfolded a page and read through the opening lines. "*Ma chèrie* Lila, so far away," he had written. "I came upon this poem today, and I thought of you." Lila felt an ache in her chest as she read through Bo's familiar slanted scrawl. He had written out a poem by Paul Éluard.

Mes rêves sont au monde
Clairs et perpétuels.
Et quand tu n'es pas là
Je rêve que je dors je rêve que je rêve.

Lila read aloud by the light of the fire, feeling the beauty of the words. "My dreams are of this world/ Clear and perpetual," she translated in a soft voice. "And when you're not here/ I dream that I sleep I dream that I dream."

Tears came to Lila's eyes, and she blinked them back. But after reading the next few lines her vision was so blurred by tears that she couldn't make out the rest of the words. Lila set down the letter and reached for her handkerchief, burying her face in the soft cloth.

She had always heard that love was painful, but she hadn't really understood what that meant until now. She hadn't realized how much it hurt to lose somebody, to build up memories with another person that nobody else would ever understand.

Lila squeezed her eyes shut and exhaled deeply. She couldn't keep torturing herself like this. There was only one solution. She had to destroy all reminders of Bo and try to put him in the past. She had to get rid of the letters.

Taking a deep breath, Lila knelt in front of the crackling fire and threw the open letter into the fireplace. The flames burst into a blaze of red and orange, licking greedily at the corners of the page. Soon the letter was completely gone.

Lila's heart contracted in pain, but she persisted in her task. One by one she fed their love letters into the fire. With each letter Bo seemed to get further and further away.

Lila threw the one remaining letter into the fire, watching sadly as the last sign of Bo went up in flames. She leaned back against a divan and grabbed a mint green throw pillow, hugging it to her chest. As Bo's intimate words crackled into smoke, she buried her head in the pillow and cried.

When the last letter had disappeared into ashes, Lila felt a strange sense of peace. And emptiness. Now Bo was really gone. It was time to start a new life. She curled up on the sofa and pulled an afghan over her body, falling into a deep sleep.

As she slept the heat grew stronger and stronger, enveloping her in its warm, comforting embrace. In her dreams the fire replaced Bo. Instead of his strong arms she had the peaceful heat of the fire, the soothing sounds of the flames crackling in the hearth.

But suddenly the heat grew unbearable, and Lila found herself choking on smoke. She felt like she was suffocating. Panicking, she tried to breathe, but her lungs filled up with thick black soot.

Lila woke up with a start, her whole body soaked in sweat. The room felt like an inferno. Something was wrong. Lila threw off her blanket and sat up, looking toward the door. Huge flames were racing into the room at lightning speed.

Lila gasped in terror and jumped up, looking around wildly for a way out. Big orange flames were licking at the door frame, and billowing black smoke was rising through the air. The smoke was so thick that she could barely see through it, and it was quickly filling up space.

Suddenly the edges of the Persian carpet caught on fire, and the flames raced along it, sizzling in their course. Lila let out a bloodcurdling scream, but the sound was muted in the smoke-filled room.

Coughing and choking, she searched desperately for an exit. The doorway was a raging inferno of flames. The only way out was through the windows.

Lila gasped for breath and put down her head, pushing her way through the thick smoke to the window on the right. But suddenly the white damask curtains in front of it went up in flames and disappeared like ghosts.

Now only one window was left. Fire was surrounding her on all sides. Feeling her chest contract in panic, Lila forced herself to stay calm. She had to get to the window across the room before the fire did.

As Lila looked for a clear course she felt her head sway. The room blurred, and the furniture seemed to tilt. Lila blinked a few times, but the room just swam before her eyes. Smoke drifted by in wavy black lines.

Suddenly the window seemed very, very far away. And her head was getting lighter and lighter. Lila gazed at the shimmering clouds in front of her, wondering why she wanted to get to the window anyway. It was actually nice and toasty in the room, and Lila was so very tired.

Lila's head spun as she squinted into the black smoke. A few bits of hot light were darting at her like flickering snakes' tongues. Lila stared back at them, mesmerized by their bright wavering dance.

But then the snakes went away. And all was black and quiet.

Chapter 2

Steven Wakefield stood outside his apartment building at Sweet Valley University early Saturday morning, tossing his bags into the trunk of his yellow Volkswagen. He was on his way home for his internship at the D.A.'s office. Although he didn't officially start work until Monday, he had to attend an orientation this afternoon.

Steven glanced down the dirt road, hoping to see Billie driving up in her blue Toyota. Even though he and Billie had already said good-bye the night before, he couldn't help hoping she would show up to say that she had changed her mind. That she didn't want to break up with him.

Billie Winkler was Steven's ex-girlfriend. He had met her when he was looking for a roommate to share his college apartment. He'd been expecting a freshman guy, not a beautiful woman with silky chestnut hair and a smile that lit up the sky. She had moved in, and they had fallen in love. They'd been together ever since.

But now it was all over between them. When Steven had broken the news to Billie that he was going home for the semester, she had been devastated.

"You're choosing work over me?" she had asked, shocked.

"What?" Steven had responded, equally surprised. "This has nothing to do with you."

"Obviously," Billie had retorted, her blue eyes clouding over in hurt.

A huge fight had ensued. Billie couldn't believe that he hadn't included her in his decision, that he hadn't even discussed the possibility with her. He didn't see what his career had to do with their relationship. He felt she should understand the wonderful opportunity he had been offered.

They had gone over the subject for hours, but neither of them would budge from their positions. They were both stubborn, a quality that had made for passionate discussions between them. "The only person I know who is more stubborn than you is *me*," Billie had remarked once affectionately. But now their obstinate natures had just brought them to an impasse.

"Well, it's your choice," Billie had said finally. "I guess you've made your preference clear."

Steven had looked at her warily. "What are you saying?" he asked in a low voice.

21

"It's me or the job," Billie said flatly. "I'm not going to just sit around and wait for you to come back to me."

Steven's mouth had dropped open. He couldn't believe she would give him an ultimatum like that. If she really loved him, she would support him in anything he did. She would be happy for him. "You're asking me to choose?" he asked, shocked.

Billie had just shrugged.

"Well, then, I choose the job," Steven said stubbornly.

"It's your loss," Billie answered quietly.

Her words had cut through Steven like a knife. He was stunned that she would give him up for a principle. Steven had always admired Billie's idealistic and headstrong nature. He had always enjoyed the challenge of her stubborn disposition. But he had never expected it to be the trait that ended their relationship.

They had continued to live together for the past month, in an atmosphere of stiff formality. They had passed each other in the hall without speaking and had avoided sharing meals together. It was like they had become strangers overnight.

Steven didn't know when he had gone through a more difficult month. At times he had longed to grab Billie in his arms and make it all better. Billie was everything he had ever dreamed of in a woman—warm, loving, intelligent, lots of fun. He couldn't bear to lose her.

But she had become an ice goddess. She was cold, sharp, and unreachable. All her tenderness was gone. Clearly she didn't love him anymore.

Last night Billie had packed a few bags and had gone to stay with a friend. "We've already said our good-bye," she had said on her way out, her voice a mixture of hurt and bitterness.

Steven had wanted to make her come back, to do something, anything, to make her smile at him once more. He was tempted to say he had changed his mind, to tell her he would stay at SVU if it would make her happy. But he knew he couldn't do that. He couldn't give up his future for her. So he had just watched her walk away—and out of his life forever.

Steven leaned against the car, his heart heavy. Even though they'd been separated for a few weeks, he still couldn't seem to digest it. He couldn't understand why they'd broken up. For a job? Was it worth it? He shook his head. How could everything go bad so fast? How could everything change overnight?

Steven slammed the trunk shut and threw one last look down the street, still hoping that Billie would show up. But all he saw was a long, empty road.

He slipped behind the wheel and drove slowly away, feeling like he was leaving his life behind.

"Steven's here!" Elizabeth exclaimed excitedly. She was peeking through the curtains in the living room, and she could see Steven's Volkswagen heading down Calico Drive. "Is everything ready?"

"I think so," Jessica said, joining her at the window.

Elizabeth hurried into the kitchen and made a final check of their preparations. The girls had decorated the walls with colorful streamers and big helium balloons. They had made Steven's favorite breakfast of blueberry pancakes and homemade walnut muffins, and the table was set. Elizabeth's Welcome Home, Bro! sign hung gaily behind it.

A key turned in the lock, and Elizabeth could hear Steven walk in the front door. The girls rushed into the foyer to greet him.

"Welcome home!" Elizabeth and Jessica called out.

"Hey, kids," Steven said softly, giving them a tired smile. A navy blue suitcase stood by his side, and a big duffel bag was slung over his shoulder.

Jessica jumped at him and gave him a big hug, but Elizabeth stood back, watching in concern. Steven looked awful. He had deep rings under his eyes, and a heavy growth of stubble darkened his strong jaw.

"Don't I get a hug from my other favorite twin?" Steven asked, shrugging his duffel bag off his shoulder and letting it drop to the floor.

Elizabeth smiled and gave him a warm hug.

Jessica tugged on Steven's hand. "Come into the kitchen," she said.

"Hey, what's all this?" Steven exclaimed as they walked into the room.

"Just a little something for you," Elizabeth said happily.

"But don't think we're making a habit of this," Jessica quipped.

Steven ruffled her hair and sat down at the table, taking in the spread appreciatively. Elizabeth ladled out warm pancakes onto their plates, and Jessica brought a pot of steaming coffee to the table.

"Mmm, my favorite. Blueberry pancakes," Steven said. He took a bite and winked at them. "Almost as good as I make myself."

"I wanted to throw a big surprise party for you, but Elizabeth wouldn't let me," Jessica declared, setting the coffeepot down on the table and pulling up a chair. She picked a muffin out of the basket in the middle of the table and nibbled at it.

Elizabeth rolled her eyes as she dripped maple syrup over her stack of pancakes. It was typical of Jessica to make her twin the enemy. Jessica didn't want to have a surprise party for Steven—she wanted an excuse to throw a big bash for all her friends. And clearly Steven wasn't in the mood for it.

"Is that right?" Steven asked. He poured himself a cup of coffee and took a sip.

"If you want, we could still have a party," Jessica put in quickly. "It's not too late. And I'm sure Mom and Dad wouldn't mind if you were here to chaperone."

She picked up her glass of orange juice and took a big gulp, gazing at him hopefully.

Steven looked down at his plate. "I don't know if I'm quite up to a party tonight, Jess."

Jessica's lips turned down in a pout. "That figures," she said.

Elizabeth narrowed her eyes, studying her older brother. Even though he was making a big show of appreciating the girls' efforts, Elizabeth didn't buy his enthusiasm. She could tell that something was bothering him. Steven looked tired and distant, and his eyes had a haunted expression in them. She bit into her pancakes thoughtfully, wondering what was wrong.

Jessica reached for her fruit cocktail and placed the parfait glass on her plate. "So is Billie going to come to visit?" she asked.

Steven shook his head slowly. "I don't know about that," he said. "I think she's pretty busy this semester." He picked up his napkin and fidgeted with it.

Elizabeth set down her fork and looked at her brother suspiciously. He was staring down at the table, intent on shredding his napkin. Steven and Billie were usually inseparable. If he came home for a weekend, she often came along with him. There was no way Billie could be too busy to see him for an entire semester. Even Jessica raised an eyebrow.

Elizabeth bit her lip, unsure if she should meddle

in his private life. But Steven looked so upset that she couldn't keep quiet. "Steven, what's wrong?" she asked softly.

"Nothing, nothing at all," Steven answered quickly, dropping the remains of his napkin on the table. He quickly cut into his stack of pancakes and brought a forkful to his lips.

Uh-oh, Jessica mouthed to Elizabeth across the table.

"Did you and Billie have a fight?" Jessica asked, scooping up a spoonful of fresh fruit.

Steven sighed and put down his fork. "Well, I guess I might as well tell you," he said. "Billie and I broke up."

"What?" Jessica exclaimed, dropping her spoon with a clatter. "You broke up?"

Elizabeth's eyes popped open in shock, and she almost choked on her juice. She put down her glass, looking at Steven in concern. No wonder her brother looked so horrible, she thought. Billie was the love of his life, and they had the perfect relationship. They had been living together all year, and Elizabeth had been sure they would get married someday.

Elizabeth touched her brother's arm lightly. "Steven, that's terrible," she said sympathetically. "You must be heartbroken."

Steven nodded and looked down, pulling slightly away from her. Elizabeth winced, feeling helpless. Her brother was obviously terribly hurt, but she didn't know what to do to make him feel better.

"What happened?" Jessica asked, leaning forward with obvious interest.

"Look, I really don't feel like talking about it," Steven mumbled. He picked up his coffee and downed the rest of the cup.

"But why in the world would you break up?" Jessica persisted. "Did you meet someone else? Did *she* meet someone else? Did you get bored with each other?"

Elizabeth shot her sister a dirty look. Steven was heartbroken, and all Jessica cared about were the gory details. She opened her mouth to intervene, but Steven held up a hand before she could get a word in.

"OK, OK, I'll tell you the story," he said. Then he looked down at the table. "Though there's really not much to tell—Billie was pretty mad that I was going away for the semester, and she didn't want to wait for me to get back."

Elizabeth was bewildered. Billie was a mature, levelheaded woman, and she was usually completely supportive of Steven. It wasn't like her to get in the way of his career. "That doesn't sound like Billie," Elizabeth ventured.

"I know," Steven said with a sigh. "She was upset because I didn't mention it to her until it was a done deal." Steven's lips turned down in a frown. "I guess it *was* pretty selfish of me. I was only thinking about myself."

Elizabeth nodded slowly. Suddenly the situation became clear. Billie had been deeply wounded that Steven hadn't shared his plans with her, so she had reacted strongly. Obviously her behavior was just a shield for her hurt. But Steven didn't see that. "It sounds more like a misunderstanding to me," Elizabeth said reassuringly. "I'm sure you'll work things out and get back together."

Steven shook his head sadly. "I don't know about that," he said. "I don't think Billie wants to have anything more to do with me."

"Well, I don't think it's bad news at all," Jessica put in. "In fact, it's a great opportunity. Now you'll have a chance to realize there are other fish in the sea." She pulled her legs up on the chair, crossed one over the other, and took a big bite out of her muffin.

"Jess!" Elizabeth whispered, sending her sister a sharp look. Sometimes she couldn't believe how thoughtless Jessica could be.

"What?" Jessica returned, a self-righteous look on her face.

"To tell you the truth, I don't really want to think about women at all right now," Steven responded.

Suddenly the telephone rang, and Steven jumped up, looking relieved. Elizabeth watched thoughtfully as he grabbed the receiver off the wall. Her brother was obviously glad to put an end to the conversation. And she didn't blame him. He had just been through a terrible breakup, and he had to endure his twin sisters' questions and a cheerful welcome home brunch. He probably just wanted to be alone.

But Steven's expression turned immediately to one of concern. His brow furrowed as he listened to the voice on the other end of the line.

Elizabeth frowned as well, feeling her heart begin to beat faster in her chest. Something was wrong. She could see it in Steven's eyes. Maybe something had happened to her parents, she thought worriedly. Maybe there had been a plane crash on the way to Chicago.

When Steven hung up, his face was grim. Elizabeth held her breath, waiting for an explanation.

"There's been a terrible fire at Fowler Crest," he announced in a solemn voice. "Lila is in the hospital. No one can locate her parents."

Elizabeth gasped, stunned at his news. A thousand questions jumped to her mind. Was Lila OK? Were her parents OK? Had the mansion been destroyed? She immediately turned to her sister in concern.

Jessica's face was ashen. She stood up, visibly shaken. "Is Lila hurt?" she asked quickly.

Steven shook his head. "I don't think her condition is serious," he said.

Elizabeth breathed a sigh of relief. But Lila wasn't the only problem. Steven had said that Mr.

and Mrs. Fowler couldn't be located. "Were her parents in the house?" she asked in a whisper.

Steven shrugged, looking worried. "I don't know."

A chill tingled up Elizabeth's spine. Scraping back her chair, she stood up quickly. "We better go to the hospital immediately," she said, her voice somber.

But Jessica already had her jacket on and was running to the front door. Elizabeth and Steven quickly followed.

Chapter 3

Lila surfaced from a deep, blank sleep to hear sounds of muted whispering around her. She struggled to open her eyes, but they refused to budge. *Somebody sewed my eyes shut,* she thought groggily. Her eyelids felt leaden, and her body seemed to weigh two tons. Sighing, she drifted back to sleep.

"Lila, wake up," a familiar female voice whispered at her side.

Groaning, Lila forced open her heavy eyelids. The room was dimly lit and smelled slightly of medicine. She squinted, trying to make out the blurry forms around her. A handsome male face was looking at her in concern. He was dark, with a strong jaw and deep brown eyes. Who was this guy?

Lila blinked and shook her fuzzy head. Slowly the figure came into clearer focus. *Oh, it's only Steven Wakefield,* she realized. And Jessica and Elizabeth were sitting at his side. What were they all doing here? she wondered. Why were they in her bedroom?

Feeling dizzy, Lila swam slowly to consciousness. *What's going on? Where am I?*

Suddenly everything came back to her. Lila remembered Bo—and the fire in the living room. She had burned all his letters, and then the whole room had gone up in flames. She had tried to get out, but then, but then . . . the rest was a void.

Lila glanced around, trying to orient herself. She was in a narrow hospital bed in a big, sterile white room. The Wakefields were sitting in wooden chairs by the bed. A huge steel apparatus was set up next to her, and a long tube was stuck in her arm, connecting her to the machine. Lila grimaced in distaste.

"What's going on?" she murmured. Her words sounded thick and distant to her ears.

Jessica squeezed her hand. "You're going to be fine, Lila," she said, her voice strong and reassuring. "There was a fire at your house, and you suffered severe smoke inhalation. But everything is OK now. You were rescued by firefighters just in the nick of time."

"But how did they find out about the fire?" Lila asked, feeling confused. "I wanted to get out the window, but it was so—far—away." Suddenly she was overtaken by a fit of coughing. Her lungs burned, and her throat felt sore and parched. Lila pulled herself up to a sitting position, wheezing and coughing wildly.

Jessica jumped up and went to the sink. She returned a moment later with a glass of water in her hands. "Here, Lila, drink this," Jessica said.

Lila blinked and took the glass from her friend. She sipped from it slowly, her eyes still tearing from her coughing attack. Finally she put down the glass, taking long, deep breaths. Her chest felt like it was still filled up with smoke.

"Hey, Li, are you OK?" Jessica asked in concern.

Lila nodded and took another deep breath, feeling her head begin to clear. The coughing fit had woken her up a bit. Sitting up straighter, she adjusted the pillows behind her back. Her hair fell in a curtain in front of her face, and she pushed it back over her shoulders. "So how did they find out about the fire?" Lila asked again.

"I guess the neighbors alerted the fire station when they saw flames coming from the house," Jessica explained.

"You're lucky to be alive," Elizabeth said softly.

"Oh, boy," Lila said worriedly. "Is the living room ruined?" Her mother would throw a fit if she learned that her newly decorated room had gone up in flames. Her parents would never trust her again.

The twins exchanged concerned glances, and Lila looked at them suspiciously.

"Yeah, it's pretty much ruined," Jessica said quietly, shifting in her seat.

"What aren't you telling me?" Lila asked.

Jessica frowned. "Well, we spoke to the doctor

when we got here. Apparently the entire west wing of the house burned down. And the rest of the house has severe smoke damage."

Lila's eyes widened in shock. The entire west wing burned down? All seven rooms? The living room, the dining room, the kitchen—her *bedroom?*

Hot tears came to her eyes, and Lila blinked them back. Was it all her fault? Had she set the house on fire? Was this the price she had to pay for burning Bo's letters?

"How . . . how did the fire start?" Lila whispered.

Elizabeth ran a finger through her hair. "Nobody seems to know yet," she responded.

Lila closed her eyes, trying to re-create the moment. She had thrown the letters in the fireplace, and then she had fallen asleep. And when she had woken up, flames were racing into the living room. Lila opened her eyes and stared vacantly at the wall, feeling thick, black guilt seep through all her pores. Obviously one of the letters had set the rug on fire. And Lila had just slept through it all. Her parents would never forgive her for this.

Then Lila frowned, feeling confused. If the fire had started in the fireplace, then it would have reached the sofa right away. But in fact the flames had come from the direction of the doorway. Lila took a ragged breath and sighed in relief. She must not be responsible for the fire after all. It must have started somewhere else in the house. But how? she wondered. Had the cook left a burner on? Had the maid left an iron plugged in?

Jessica touched her arm, and Lila looked at her distractedly. "Uh, Lila, your parents," she began. She coughed slightly and cleared her throat. "The authorities haven't been able to get in touch with your parents."

Lila scowled. "That's because they're not around."

Jessica exhaled deeply, looking visibly relieved. "Thank goodness for that," she murmured. She stood up and walked to the window, drawing back the curtains and letting a ray of morning sunshine into the dark room. The blue-green Pacific Ocean sparkled in the distance.

Lila blinked, suddenly realizing why her best friend had sounded so worried. "You thought something had happened to my parents," she said softly.

Jessica turned and faced her, tears shining in her eyes. "We didn't know," she said, shrugging nonchalantly.

Lila blinked back tears as well, touched by Jessica's concern. "They're on vacation on a remote island in the South Pacific," she said. She plumped a pillow behind her back and shifted slightly.

Jessica turned and looked at her, an expression of surprise on her face. "They are?" she asked. "Since when?"

Lila shrugged. "It was a spur-of-the-moment decision," she explained. "My parents decided they needed a break and just took off yesterday." Lila scowled again, feeling abandoned. Sometimes she felt as if her parents were children and she was the adult.

"How can we contact them?" Steven asked, pulling his chair closer to the side of the bed.

Lila shook her head. "We can't," she said flatly. "The island doesn't have a single phone. They chose it specifically for its privacy and isolation."

Steven's eyes narrowed worriedly. "That's unfortunate," he said quietly. "Is there somebody who can take care of financial matters for the estate while they're away?"

Lila sighed. "Yeah, there's a lawyer for the estate. And the mansion's insured."

"Well, that's good," Steven said. "So the lawyer could oversee the reconstruction of the estate while your parents are out of town?"

Lila nodded, the word *reconstruction* reverberating in her head. Suddenly the magnitude of the situation hit her, and she laid her head back on the pillow. Now she was really and truly all alone. She had lost her boyfriend, her home, and all her belongings. And her parents were far, far away.

Lila closed her eyes in pain, plunged even deeper into the despair she had felt when she was burning Bo's letters. She saw them catching fire in her mind's eye—and pictured the flames ripping through her house and her life.

"Love can ruin everything," she whispered dramatically.

Steven brushed her hand with his own. "I know

what you mean," he said sympathetically.

Lila looked at him quickly to see if he was kidding. But he was looking at her intently, a serious expression on his face. Lila frowned, wondering what had come over Jessica's older brother. She had known Steven for years, but they had barely exchanged more than five words. He had never seemed to notice her before, let alone be concerned about her. And now he was staring at her with troubled eyes. Lila shook her head. Square, conservative Steven Wakefield was getting sentimental? What was going on?

Feeling uncomfortable under Steven's intense gaze, Lila gave him a weak smile and pulled her arm away.

Jessica shot her brother a dirty look. "Lila, don't worry," she said as she crossed the room. "Just relax and get better. You're going to be just fine." She sat down on the bed by Lila's side.

"Just fine," Lila murmured, repeating Jessica's words. She wondered what that really meant.

A nurse in a white uniform entered the room. He was young and slight, with dark brown hair and a kind-looking face. A fresh stack of towels was tucked under his arm.

He gave Lila a gentle smile. "How are you feeling?" he asked.

"Tired," Lila responded.

"OK, I think visiting hours are over for the day," he said, turning a switch on Lila's IV. He smiled at the

Wakefields. "You should let Lila get back to sleep," he said softly. "She's been through a really rough time."

The twins stood up after the nurse had left. "Well, it looks like you're in good hands," Jessica said.

Lila shrugged nonchalantly. "Only the best for Lila Fowler," she remarked, feeling jaded. "After all, this is Fowler Memorial Hospital."

Sweet Valley's main hospital was named after Lila's great-uncle, so Lila was sure to get special treatment. As it was, she had been given a huge corner room with a view of the ocean. But right now none of her privileges seemed to matter. And Lila had a feeling that they would never matter to her again.

"We'll stop by tomorrow," Jessica said, putting a hand on Lila's arm.

Lila nodded and rested her head on the pillow. As the painkillers dripped into her arm she felt herself slipping back into a foggy sleep.

Steven felt his pulse pick up as he walked into the District Attorney's office in downtown Sweet Valley later that afternoon. Even though it was a Saturday, the place was buzzing with activity. The office was small and dark, with lots of rickety wooden desks jammed together. Phones were jangling off the hook, and a constant stream of people seemed to be walking in and out the door.

Steven stood back for a moment, breathing in the charged atmosphere. He had always dreamed of working in a place like this. It was gritty and tough, and excitement hung palpably in the air. *Maybe someday I'll be a D.A. myself,* Steven thought. *Maybe I'll be in charge of an office like this.*

Pulling himself out of his reverie, he walked up to the front desk and introduced himself to the receptionist. She was a middle-aged woman with silver-streaked dark brown hair and bright blue eyes. A complicated telephone system was hooked up in front of her, and a steady stream of paper was pouring out of a fax machine on the side of the desk.

"Hi, Steven," she said, smiling warmly. "I'm Adele." She pulled out a directory and ran her index finger down a list of names. "I believe you should go see Jason Mann," she said. "He's in charge of the interns." She pointed toward a desk at the opposite end of the office.

Steven thanked her and headed across the noisy room, feeling his adrenaline soar in the pulsing environment. He was thrilled to be starting work at last. He had been looking forward to this day for months. When he reached the other side of the room, Steven stopped in front of a solid oak desk against the far wall. A balding man was hunched behind it, talking a mile a minute into the phone. "Put Jake on the case," he barked out finally. "Send him to court today." He hung up the phone abruptly.

Steven cleared his throat, shifting uncomfortably. Suddenly he felt like he was just in the way. These people had important work to do for the city of Sweet Valley. He was just a freshman college student with no experience in law.

"What can I do for you?" the man asked abruptly.

"Uh, I'm Steven Wakefield," Steven responded nervously. "The new intern."

The man squinted. "An intern, eh? All right. Have a seat. I'll ring Joe Garrison."

Steven sat down in one of the straight-backed wooden chairs against the wall, feeling anxious. Joe Garrison was the District Attorney himself. Steven hadn't realized he would be working for him directly.

Suddenly the door next to him opened, and a small, tough-looking man came out. He had close-cropped, dark curly hair and keen, deep blue eyes.

"Steven Wakefield?" he asked.

Steven nodded and stood up quickly, holding out his hand.

"Joe Garrison," the D.A. said, shaking Steven's hand firmly. "Come into my office. We've got a tough case for you."

Steven's chest tightened in excitement as he followed Mr. Garrison into the office. The space was dimly lit and cluttered. Mountains of important-looking documents covered a huge black desk, and file folders were lined up on every available surface. A computer stood in the corner of the desk, along with a fax machine and a printer.

The D.A. slouched into a black leather swivel

chair and waved Steven into a seat across from the desk. "You've heard about the Fowler Crest fire?" he asked without preamble.

Steven nodded. "The accident's been all over the papers today."

"Well, it wasn't an accident," Mr. Garrison said, leaning back and lighting a cigar.

Steven blinked in shock. "It wasn't?"

Mr. Garrison took a puff. "Nope," he said. "Gasoline traces were found all over the estate." He tapped his cigar on the edge of a big silver ashtray in the middle of the desk. "Which makes this the first big case of arson to hit Sweet Valley in years."

"And not necessarily the last," Steven put in, thinking back to what he had learned about arson in his prelaw course last semester. Apparently arsonists were like serial killers. They tended to work in cycles. "Arsonists rarely hit just once."

Joe Garrison smiled for the first time, looking impressed. "Exactly. So that's why we've got to nip this in the bud."

Steven felt his pulse speed up. He had imagined he would be indirectly involved in some casework, but he had thought his job would consist mostly of doing errands and taking care of paperwork. He had never dreamed he would be helping out on a really important case right from the start.

The D.A. swiveled his chair around and leaned forward, resting his elbows on his desk. "Do you know the Fowler girl, Lila?" he asked.

"As a matter of fact, I do," Steven said. "She's a friend of the family." But as he spoke, he realized that he didn't know Lila at all. He thought of how she had looked at the hospital earlier—fragile and vulnerable and in pain. He had always thought Lila was one of Jessica's more superficial friends, but he had felt real sympathy for her this morning.

"Well, you're going to get to know Lila even better," Mr. Garrison said. "You're going to get to know everything about her." He put out his cigar and leaned back in his chair.

Steven frowned, unsure of Lila's relevance to the case. He didn't quite see how an investigation of Lila would help them find the arsonist. "In order to find out who might want to do this to her and her family?" Steven ventured.

"No, to find out why Lila might do this to herself," Mr. Garrison answered.

"What?" Steven gasped in shock.

His boss sat back in his leather chair and tapped his fingertips lightly together. "When Lila was brought into the hospital, traces of sulfur were detected on her fingertips and matches were found in her pocket," he explained. "The girl had been playing with fire."

Steven's mouth dropped open. He couldn't believe it. Had the whole scene in the hospital been an act? Did Lila actually try to burn the whole house down? And had she wanted to go up in flames with it? "But . . . but why would Lila set fire to her own house?" Steven asked. "It doesn't make sense."

Mr. Garrison shrugged. "Maybe not," he said. "But if there's a reason, we're going to find it. Your mission is to get to know everything about Lila Fowler. *Everything.*"

"OK, dinner's ready," Jessica announced later that evening, carrying a big bowl of sticky white rice to the table and setting it down next to a platter of warm egg rolls. She and Elizabeth had prepared a meal of Chinese stir-fry while Steven was at work.

Elizabeth followed her with a heaping dish of steamed vegetables and placed it in the middle of the table. Steven collected their plates and ladled spoonfuls of rice and vegetables onto them while Jessica grabbed a glass pitcher and filled it with ice water.

Jessica sighed as she sat down at the table. "I'm really glad we're having this intimate little dinner instead of a huge party," she muttered sarcastically under her breath. She reached for a small egg roll and popped it into her mouth whole.

Elizabeth gave her a sharp look. "Jessica! You wouldn't want to have a celebration while your best friend was in the hospital."

Jessica shrugged and swallowed. "Why not? She's OK. Lila doesn't want everyone sitting around feeling sorry for her." She picked up her napkin and wiped off her mouth.

44

"Oh, really?" Steven asked, looking suddenly interested. "So Lila's the strong, self-sufficient type?"

Jessica nodded. "Definitely," she asserted, feeling proud of her best friend. "Lila doesn't let anything get her down." She picked up a bottle of soy sauce and turned it upside down, letting the thin liquid drip slowly over her vegetables.

Steven nodded. "I wonder if that's just a facade," he said, adding some rice to his plate.

Jessica shrugged and lifted a forkful of food to her mouth.

"She hasn't been through anything particularly difficult lately?" Steven persisted.

Elizabeth gave him an odd look. "Since when are you so interested in Lila?" she asked, reaching across the table for the soy sauce.

"Since I've been assigned to her case," Steven responded.

"What?" Jessica and Elizabeth exclaimed in unison.

"I've been assigned to investigate the Fowler Crest fire for the D.A.'s office," Steven explained. He dipped his fork into his plate and took a big bite of his steamed vegetables.

"What an unbelievable opportunity!" Elizabeth exclaimed, dripping sauce over her food. "This has got to be one of the most important cases in Sweet Valley at the moment."

Steven nodded. "It is pretty exciting," he agreed. "So that's why I need to know everything about Lila and her family."

"Well, there's not a lot to know," Jessica remarked lightly. "They're rich, and they travel a lot."

Steven's eyes narrowed. "There might be more to it than that," he said. "It seems a little odd for a sixteen-year-old girl to be home all alone with no way to contact her parents whatsoever."

Jessica shrugged. "Lila's pretty independent." She drank down her entire glass of water and grabbed for the pitcher in the middle of the table.

"Is she close to her father?" Steven asked. He reached for an egg roll and took a bite out of it.

"He's not at home very much, is he?" Elizabeth put in, a thoughtful look on her face. She took a last bite of her food. Then she leaned back and crossed one leg over the other.

"No, he's always flying around the world, taking care of business for his computer chip company," Jessica affirmed.

Steven nodded, obviously digesting all the information. "And her mother?"

"Her mother's name is Grace, and Lila just sort of found her again," Jessica said, pushing away her plate. She sat back in her chair and pulled her knees up to her chest. "Her parents were divorced for years. Lila grew up with her father. Her mother was living in Paris with her boyfriend—some French guy named Pierre. But then she came home to visit Lila, and she and Mr. Fowler fell in love again. So they had that huge wedding and flew off on a second honeymoon."

"And everything ended up happily ever after," Steven finished for her, squinting thoughtfully just like Mr. Wakefield did when he was on a big case. Jessica could see her brother's mind clicking as he filed away the information.

The teapot began to whistle, and Elizabeth jumped up to get it. She returned to the table a moment later with a pot of fresh mint tea and biscuits.

Steven grabbed a biscuit and munched on it. "Has Lila been through any traumas?" he asked.

Jessica pondered the question. "Well, there was that incident with John Pfeifer, the sports editor at the *Oracle*—" she began.

The John Pfeifer story certainly counted as a trauma, Jessica reflected. Lila had gone out with him on a date, and he had attacked her violently in the car. Fortunately Lila had escaped, but it had taken her months to recover from the ordeal.

"What incident?" Steven asked quickly.

Jessica hesitated, feeling torn. She wanted to help Steven, but she didn't think Lila would appreciate it if Jessica revealed her best friend's private life to him. She looked quickly to her sister for guidance. Elizabeth gave her a small shake of her head.

Elizabeth's right, Jessica realized. Even if the information would be useful for the case, Jessica couldn't betray Lila's confidence. "Just . . . just a difficult incident," she finished lamely.

"Jess, that doesn't tell me much," Steven said.

47

He picked up the teapot and filled up their cups.

"Steven, it really is a private matter," Elizabeth put in. She picked up her teacup and blew on it softly.

"I'm sorry, but I can't say any more," Jessica added. "Lila will have to tell you about it herself if she wants to." She reached across the table for a biscuit.

Steven nodded, taking a sip of tea. "It's OK. I understand."

"But I don't understand," Elizabeth interjected. "What does Lila's personal life have to do with the accident last night?" she asked.

"That's exactly what I asked the D.A.," Steven said. Elizabeth's eyes widened. "And?"

"It turns out the fire was arson," Steven said grimly.

"Arson!" Jessica echoed in shock.

Steven nodded solemnly.

A chill raced down Jessica's spine at Steven's words. The situation was much more serious than she had realized. This wasn't about Lila's property. It was about her *life*. Somebody had tried to hurt her best friend. And whoever it was, he—or *she*— was still out there.

Suddenly Jessica felt terribly worried about Lila.

Chapter 4

Devon pulled off to the side of the road on Sunday morning, feeling a strange mixture of apprehension and hope. The sun was beginning to rise and cast a slanting ray on the empty Midwest highway. Sitting back in his seat, Devon pulled out his worn road map and studied it. He squinted at the sign ahead of him. Exit 33. Clearwater, Ohio. This was it.

Devon yawned and stretched. He had driven for ten hours straight the day before and had spent the past two nights in lumpy hotel beds. He was looking forward to a shower and a good night's sleep.

Devon revved the engine and turned onto the exit ramp, passing signs for a rest stop and a shopping mall. His cousins' suburban Ohio town looked nothing like his old town in Connecticut. The landscape was strangely flat, and the houses were small and uniform. Except for a few open convenience stores and gas stations, the town seemed to be still asleep. The only sounds of life came from a few distant lawn mowers and the chirping of birds in the trees.

Devon passed a small park and turned onto Maple Lane, unable to prevent a quick tightening in his chest. He recognized the street from his visits during childhood, and it seemed to be completely unchanged. *Maybe I'll finally find the kind of home I never had,* he thought as he coasted down the tree-lined street.

Aunt Peggy, Uncle Mark, and their children, Ross and Allan, had always seemed like the perfect, loving family to him. Maybe they weren't wildly exciting or unusual, but it was their very normalcy that had always appealed to Devon— their stability, their straw welcome mat, their Sunday night family dinners.

Devon pulled up in front of the Wilsons' house, looking at it thoughtfully. The residence was just as he had remembered it—a small, redbrick, split-level house with square windows. A white picket fence surrounded the well-kept grass, and a rickety old swing set sat on the front lawn.

As Devon turned off his motorcycle, the front door flew open and the whole family hurried outside to greet him. Devon slid off his bike and grabbed his backpack, slinging it over his shoulder.

Aunt Peggy rushed down the front walk ahead

of everybody. She had pale skin and puffy reddish brown hair wrapped up on top of her head in a chignon. Her arms were outstretched, and tears of sympathy sparkled in her light blue eyes. "Oh, you poor boy," she said, enveloping him in a maternal embrace. "We're so sorry about your parents."

Devon hugged her, feeling somewhat awkward. He wasn't used to public displays of affection.

"Welcome, son!" Uncle Mark boomed. He was a burly man with a stubbly face and a slight beer belly. Uncle Mark was a housing contractor and spent much of his time working at home. He held out a solid hand and shook Devon's hand firmly.

"Hey, Devon," his cousin Ross said, looking slightly intimidated. Ross was a gangly fourteen-year-old with longish, straight brown hair and light blue eyes. He was wearing faded jeans and a red flannel shirt.

"How you doin', Ross?" Devon responded, pulling off his helmet and setting it on the seat.

Allan just stood to the side. A cute eleven-year-old boy with red hair and freckles, he was the one Devon had always preferred. Allan was more playful and innocent than his older brother. When they were younger, Devon had taught him to ride a bike. Devon smiled at him, and Allan grinned back, revealing a chipped front tooth.

"You're just in time for Aunt Peggy's special flapjack breakfast," Uncle Mark said.

"And this won't be the last," Aunt Peggy told

him, smiling warmly. "Our home is your home."

"Hey, Devon, will you take me for a ride on your motorcycle this afternoon?" Allan asked eagerly, bouncing by his side as they walked toward the house.

"Sure," Devon said, feeling unexpected tears come to his eyes. Maybe he had found what he was looking for after all.

"The visiting committee is here!" Jessica called out as she and Elizabeth walked into Lila's hospital room on Sunday evening. Jessica staggered through the door, her arms laden with supplies for Lila. Taking a deep breath, she set a small brown grocery bag on the table and dropped the rest of her stuff on the floor.

Jessica shook out her wet hair and hung up her jean jacket on a hook, shivering slightly. It had been misty all day, and she and Elizabeth had gotten caught in a sudden downpour in the parking lot.

Lila's eyes widened. "Did you guys take a shower outside?" she asked.

Elizabeth nodded ruefully. "Something like that." She shrugged off her black raincoat and hung it up next to Jessica's jacket. Then she headed for the bathroom. "I'll be right back," she said. "I just want to get cleaned up."

Lila nodded and turned to Jessica. "You're just in time for dinner," she said dryly. She was sitting up in bed in a blue hospital gown, a tray of food set

52

out in front of her. Lila's light brown hair hung loose around her shoulders, and she wore a plastic ID bracelet around her wrist. A number of fashion magazines were scattered about the bed.

"And dessert!" Jessica said, fishing through the grocery bag and pulling out a pint of Casey's ice cream. She plopped it down on the tray with a flourish. They had brought Million Dollar Mocha, Lila's favorite flavor.

Lila smiled weakly. "How did you manage to sneak that in?" she asked.

Jessica grinned. "We have our ways." She pulled the lid off the ice cream and stuck a plastic spoon in it. "There was a cute orderly at the desk."

Lila shook her head in mock disapproval. "I should have known," she said. "You flirted your way in."

Jessica's blue-green eyes twinkled as she took a seat on the side of Lila's bed. "I have to admit, I think we charmed him," she agreed. "He didn't even ask to look at our bags."

Elizabeth walked back into the room, rubbing a towel through her hair. Wrapping it turban style around her head, she took a seat in the chair by the bed. "How are you feeling?" she asked.

"I'm OK," Lila responded, shrugging. "A little tired."

Jessica sat down by her side, glancing at her best friend worriedly. Lila looked awful. Her face was pale, and her eyes were red and puffy.

Jessica nudged at the bags on the floor, hoping to cheer up her friend. "You look great in that blue gown and everything, but I brought you some clothes just in case you feel like a change. And some toiletries as well," she said. She reached for a cosmetic case and placed it on the night table. Fishing in the bag, she pulled out some hair accessories and spread them out next to the case.

"Thanks, Jess," Lila said, giving her a grateful smile. A crash of thunder rocked the sky, and the sounds of rain pelting steadily down enveloped the dark room. The waves of the foamy blue-gray ocean billowed in the distance.

Lila shivered, pulling her gown tighter around her. "This weather is depressing," she said.

"Well, why don't we have a fashion show to brighten things up?" Jessica suggested, plopping a fat floral overnight bag on the bed and unzipping it. Picking it up, she dumped the contents on the bed. "Do you want to see what I brought?" she asked.

"No, thanks," Lila said with a lackluster attitude. "I'm sure everything is fine." She didn't even bother glancing at the clothes. Jessica bit her lip, exchanging a concerned glance with her sister. Slinging a few dresses over her arm, she stood up and headed for the closet.

"Where's Amy?" Lila asked, sounding vulnerable. "I would have thought she'd come to visit." A slim, blond cheerleader, Amy Sutton was a good friend of Lila and Jessica. The girls formed a notorious threesome at Sweet Valley High.

Jessica turned from the closet, where she was hanging up the last dress. "She's in Colorado visiting her cousins, remember?" she said.

Lila nodded. "Oh, that's right."

Jessica headed back to the bed and took a seat by Lila's side. "Why don't you eat something?" she suggested.

Jessica lifted the lid off the plastic container sitting on Lila's lap. It held some rubbery chicken and white rice, plus a gelatinous thing that resembled Jell-O. Jessica recoiled at the sight of it.

"Oh, gross!" Lila exclaimed. "This stuff is worse than airplane food." She poked her fork into the chicken, her nose crumpled up in distaste. Then she pushed away the plate. "I can't wait to get out of here." Flicking her hair back over her shoulders, she lifted a spoonful of ice cream to her mouth.

"You really should eat some dinner first," Elizabeth said, reminding Jessica of their mother. "You need to get back your strength." She unwrapped her towel and hung it over the back of her chair. Shaking her head, she fluffed out her hair.

Lila shrugged. "I'll eat properly as soon as I get home," she said. "Ferdinand can make me one of his gourmet dinners." Lila leaned over to set the tray on her bedside table, holding the carton of ice cream in her hand. "After all, the kitchen is in the east wing." She dipped her spoon in the ice cream and took a big scoop.

Elizabeth glanced at Jessica. Jessica stared down at her lap, fidgeting with her hands. She didn't know how to break the news to Lila that she couldn't go home. The last thing she wanted to do was upset her best friend further with the news that the fire was arson. But then, she really had no choice. Lila needed to be aware of the situation.

Jessica drew a deep breath. "Lila, there's something you should know about the fire."

Lila sighed, taking another spoonful of ice cream. "What? Did the whole house actually burn down?"

Jessica shook her head, shifting uncomfortably. "It turns out that the fire was an act of arson," she said quietly. A clap of thunder shook the room, seeming to accentuate her words.

The color drained from Lila's face. "What?" she whispered in shock. "Are you sure?" The carton of ice cream fell soundlessly into her lap, and Elizabeth quickly retrieved it, setting it on the night table.

Jessica nodded grimly. "Apparently there were gasoline traces all over the estate."

"Somebody tried to burn the mansion down?" Lila asked, an expression of disbelief on her face. "But . . . but why would anyone want to do that?"

Elizabeth shook her head. "We don't know," she said softly.

Lila was silent as she digested the information. "This is devastating," she said finally, leaning back against her pillows. Tears came to her eyes, and she blinked them back. "I wish my parents were here," she whispered.

Jessica laid a comforting hand over her friend's. "We're here, Li," she said. "And your parents will be back in no time."

Lila nodded and gave them a slight smile. "You're right," she said. "I'm sure I'll feel better when I get out of here." She grabbed a tissue out of the box on her night table and blew her nose.

"Are they going to let you out soon?" Elizabeth asked, replacing the cover of Lila's uneaten dinner.

Lila nodded. "I'm going to be discharged tomorrow." She reached for a barrette lying on the night table.

"And you'll stay with us until your parents get back," Jessica said reassuringly. "I'll come pick you up tomorrow after school."

But Lila shook her head. "No, I want to go home," she said. She pulled back her hair and tied it adeptly in a knot at the nape of her neck, fastening it with the barrette.

"But you can't," Jessica protested. "It's too dangerous."

"I don't care," Lila said in a firm voice. "It's bad enough that I lost almost everything I have. I don't want to feel further uprooted by staying in someone else's house."

Jessica bit her lip. She was terrified by the idea of Lila staying alone. She didn't want to scare her best friend, but Lila might be in serious danger. After all, whoever set the house on fire could still be around. And maybe they would be back.

Well, Jessica decided, she would make another stab at it tomorrow. Maybe Lila would change her mind when she realized she didn't have much of a home anymore. And if Lila still refused, then Jessica would just have to stay with her.

A young nurse wearing white pants and a blue cap tapped on the door and walked in the room. She had bright green eyes and thick blond hair that curled up at the bottom.

"Time for your medicine!" the nurse said cheerily. She poured some cherry liquid onto a spoon and fed it to Lila. "Mmm!" she said encouragingly.

The nurse straightened the sheets and plumped up Lila's pillows, leaning over to pick up the dinner tray on her way out of the room.

Lila rolled her eyes when she was gone. "You would think I was three years old," she said. "Or that I had lost all my mental capacities along with my belongings."

Another crash of thunder rocked the sky, and a bolt of lightning followed. Raindrops pelted the window.

"Well, at least there's something positive in all this," Jessica declared, standing up and stretching. She went to the window and shut the curtains.

"What's that?" Lila asked, drawing her knees up to her chest and wrapping her arms around them.

Jessica walked back to the bed. "Losing so much stuff is a great excuse for a massive shopping spree," she said. "We can go shopping for days to replace your wardrobe and your bedroom furniture."

But Lila looked even sadder at her words. "I don't think I'm up for shopping, Jess."

Jessica frowned and looked at her best friend carefully. Lila always wanted to go shopping. Obviously she was doing very, very badly.

Elizabeth sighed as she and Jessica walked out of the room. She had never been very close to Lila, but she really felt for her now. She couldn't imagine what it would be like to lose your home and all your belongings. And to deal with it alone too. Given the circumstances, Lila was doing very well.

The girls reached the elevator bank, and Elizabeth punched the button, chewing on her lower lip while they waited. Not only was she worried about Lila, she was also concerned about Steven. She had never seen him look so miserable. Usually her brother was bustling with energy and good humor, but now he was gloomy and serious. Elizabeth felt completely powerless. She wished she could do something to make Lila and Steven feel better.

The glass doors opened, and a group of young

male interns in blue uniforms walked out. The girls got in, and Jessica pressed the button for the lobby, her expression downcast. Her sister was obviously upset as well, Elizabeth thought. She didn't even notice the cute doctors. Jessica was strangely silent as they rode down to the first floor. Usually she burst into chatter the moment they were alone. But now she was just slumped against the wall, hugging her jean jacket to her chest.

"Hey, Jess, are you OK?" Elizabeth asked as they walked out of the elevator.

"Yeah, I'm OK," Jessica responded with a sigh. She slung her jacket over her arm and pushed an errant strand of hair out of her face. "I'm just really worried about Lila staying all alone in the mansion."

"I know—me too," Elizabeth said, her low pumps clicking in the smooth, long white corridor. "But I think she might change her mind when she sees the place. After all, the bedrooms were all destroyed. Lila doesn't even have anywhere to sleep."

Jessica nodded. "Actually, the damage wasn't as bad as they originally thought. Last night on the phone, Lila told me the police report said that some of the structure was still intact, but that there was severe damage. But she has no idea which rooms were hit worst. I'm just worried she'll get her hopes up for no reason."

"Still, it's normal that she wants to go home," Elizabeth added. "Her parents are away, and she's in the hospital. Fowler Crest is all she's got at the moment."

"Yeah, I guess you're right," Jessica conceded.

The girls crossed the lobby and pushed through the glass doors into the parking lot. The rain was falling lightly now, and Elizabeth took deep breaths of the cool evening air. It was a relief to be outside after the suffocating atmosphere of the antiseptic hospital.

Jessica shrugged into her jacket and buttoned it up. "You know, I've never seen Lila seem so down," she said. "She's not acting like herself at all. She has no interest in shopping whatsoever." Jessica squinted thoughtfully into the rain. "Do you think maybe the smoke inhalation affected her brain?"

"Don't worry," Elizabeth said, trying to reassure her sister. "She'll come around. She's probably just in shock at the moment."

Jessica didn't look convinced. She just scowled and kicked at the wet gravel with the toe of her tennis shoe.

Elizabeth wrapped her raincoat tightly around her and tied the belt at the waist. "C'mon, you know Lila," Elizabeth said. "She never says no to shopping. And there's nobody better to take her on her therapeutic rounds of conspicuous consumerism than you."

"That's true," Jessica agreed, putting down her head and walking into the drizzle.

"After all, what are friends for?" Elizabeth asked. She slung an arm around her sister's shoulders as they crossed the gravel parking lot. "Jess, you're a good pal."

Jessica rolled her eyes. "Very funny, Liz," she said. "But at least it's something I can do for her."

Elizabeth nodded. "I know. I'm just teasing."

The girls reached the Jeep, and Elizabeth ducked into the driver's seat, deep in thought. Jessica had just given her an idea. Maybe there *was* a way the twins could help Lila *and* Steven. Maybe they could make a difference after all.

Elizabeth turned on the engine and flicked on the windshield wipers. Glancing over her shoulder to make sure nobody was behind them, she backed out of the misty lot carefully. Then she turned onto the main road, feeling some of her energy return to her. "Jess, I've got a plan," Elizabeth declared.

Jessica pulled the seat belt across her chest and snapped it into place. "Shoot."

"Operation Cheer Up," Elizabeth said. "We'll be the happiness committee."

Jessica made a face. "What is this? Are we the Red Cross?" She wriggled down in her seat and put her feet up on the dashboard.

Elizabeth shrugged. "Something like that," she said. "You take care of Lila, and I'll work on cheering up Steven."

"And just how are you planning to do that?" Jessica asked.

Elizabeth steered the car onto Valley Crest Drive. "By making sure he's not too lonely, that he's not spending too much time by himself or drowning himself in his work," Elizabeth explained. "In fact, I'll invite him to hang out with me and Todd tonight—a good video and a carton of mint cookie ice cream can do wonders for a broken heart."

"What a cozy threesome," Jessica scoffed. "Liz, Steven doesn't need to hang out with old married couples. He needs to meet other women. That's the only way he's going to get over Billie and get on with his life."

Elizabeth shook her head. "Steven is totally in love with Billie," she countered. "Can't you see that? He needs some family TLC and a chance to make up with her."

"Nothing better than sharing an exciting night with Liz and Todd to make you want to run back to your significant other," Jessica said dryly.

But Elizabeth just laughed, feeling her spirits rise for the first time in days. She couldn't wait to put her plan into motion. Her big brother would be back to his old self in no time. "You know, Jess, some people actually *like* hanging out with their families," she pointed out with a smile. "Not everyone is out looking for Mr. Tall, Dark, and Mysterious."

For the first time that evening Jessica laughed as well. "Who says he has to be dark?" she asked.

✦ ✦ ✦

"Devon, would you like some more turkey?" Aunt Peggy asked on Sunday evening at the dinner table.

"Sure," Devon agreed, passing her his plate.

It was a traditional Sunday dinner at the Wilsons', and the whole family was eating together. They were having a feast of roasted turkey and mashed potatoes. There was even fresh apple pie for dessert. Devon couldn't remember the last time he had sat down for a family meal.

"Hey, Ross, you wanna play catch tonight?" Allan asked, making vertical track marks in his mashed potatoes with the side of a fork. Obviously he was a big baseball fan. He was wearing a Chicago Cubs T-shirt and a navy blue baseball cap turned around backward. A few strands of red hair peeked out of the hat.

Ross shook his head and scowled. "Nah, I gotta study for a chemistry test."

"Why don't you ask Devon to help you?" Aunt Peggy suggested, setting a basket of warm buns in the middle of the table. "Devon has been tested at the genius level in physics and the general sciences."

Devon stared down at his plate, his cheeks burning. He didn't know how she'd gotten that information, but he wished she had kept it to herself. He was sick of hearing people talk about his high IQ and his talent for the sciences. Back in

Connecticut his fellow students had just envied him for it, and the faculty had only been interested in using him to win prizes for the school.

Ross looked at him eagerly. "That would be great!" he exclaimed. "Devon, would you mind?"

"Sure, no problem," Devon said, still feeling the prickly heat in his cheeks. He cut into his turkey and took a big bite, staring at his plate fixedly as he chewed.

"Aww, you don't wanna play catch?" Allan complained. He grabbed a roll from the basket and bobbed it in the air with his left hand.

Devon smiled, relieved that Allan had changed the subject. "Tell you what. Why don't we play catch for an hour while Ross does his homework? That way it'll still be light enough to play and then Ross and I can go over his chemistry assignment this evening."

"Awesome!" Allan exclaimed, a big grin on his face. He split open the roll and spread butter over it with his knife.

"Hey, thanks, Devon," Ross added.

"Sure," Devon said, trying not to let his pleasure show. He had never had any siblings, and for the first time in his life he felt like a big brother. *Ross and Allan don't realize how lucky they are,* Devon thought. *They don't know how unusual it is to be normal.*

Aunt Peggy began clearing the table, and Devon jumped up to help her. He stacked up the dinner plates and carried them to the sink. Opening the dishwasher, he began loading them in.

Aunt Peggy put her hands on her hips, her mouth wide open. "Boys, do you see this?" she asked. "Devon is actually helping with the dishes without me even having to *ask.*"

Ross grinned. "I bet that will last about a week."

Devon shut the dishwasher and sat back down at the table. The boys were ripping pieces off their paper napkins and shooting spitballs at each other. Moments later Aunt Peggy carried a warm apple pie to the table. Uncle Mark followed with a carton of vanilla ice cream. The sweet smell of the freshly baked dessert filled the air.

As Devon took his first forkful of apple pie, a warm glow came over him. He was really beginning to feel that he belonged. It was like a dream come true. He had wanted to be a part of a close-knit family like this forever.

After they were finished with dessert, Aunt Peggy brought a teapot to the table. She poured cups of tea for herself and Uncle Mark, looking at Devon questioningly. Devon shook his head, and the kids jumped up to leave the table.

"Whoa! Hold it one minute!" Uncle Mark said, holding up a hand. "Tonight we're having a family conference."

Ross and Allan groaned and sat back in their seats.

"Devon, we thought you might like to talk about your future," Uncle Mark began.

"We don't know what your plans are, but we want you to know you're welcome to stay with us for as long as you'd like," Aunt Peggy said, taking a sip of tea.

"You could even stay here through college if you want," Uncle Mark added. "That is, if you decide to go to Ohio State University."

Devon's eyes widened. He couldn't believe they were making such a generous offer. And it was just his first day here. It seemed too good to be true.

Feeling a bit uneasy, Devon cleared his throat. "Well, actually I'm seeking a guardian," he said slowly. "My father stated in—"

"Oh, we know that already," Aunt Peggy said, interrupting him with a wave of her hand. "We know all about the will and the inheritance."

Devon blinked, a little taken aback. He had thought the contents of the will were strictly confidential. "Um, how did you find out about it?" he asked.

"One of the lawyers for the estate contacted us," Aunt Peggy explained. "Since you're a minor, the judge was concerned about your well-being." Aunt Peggy smiled. "She thought our home would be an appropriate place for you."

Devon bit his lip, feeling like his privacy had been invaded. He wondered if all his relatives were privy to the information now.

"We're thrilled that you've chosen us," Aunt Peggy went on. She propped her elbows on the table and rested her chin on her hands, giving Devon a warm, dreamy smile.

"What's ours is yours," Uncle Mark said. He leaned back comfortably in his chair, taking a big gulp of tea.

"Even though our home is modest, of course," Aunt Peggy put in.

"And *boring*," Ross added. "We don't have any motorcycles or cool leather jackets."

"Clothes and the motorcycles don't mean much," Devon remarked offhandedly. "Money is easy to come by. A real home is a lot more difficult to find."

"It *would* be easier if we had more room for you," Aunt Peggy said, standing up and stacking up dishes. "And then, of course, there's the leaky roof."

Devon's eyes widened at her words. She seemed to be taking his remark as an offer.

"I'm sure that Barbara from my French class would agree to go out on a date with me if I picked her up on a motorcycle like Devon's," Ross put in.

"If you get a motorcycle, then I get a mountain bike!" Allan yelled out.

Ross's lips turned down in a scowl. "Why are you always trying to copy me?" he asked, flinging a roll at his brother. The roll hit Allan in the chest and bounced onto the table.

Allan retrieved it quickly and took aim. "I am not! You always get everything 'cause you're older, and it's not fair."

Allan whipped the roll back at his brother, and Ross ducked, snickering at him. The roll hit the kitchen counter and fell to the floor.

"Boys! Boys!" Aunt Peggy interrupted, standing up with her hands on her hips. "Watch your manners! We've got a guest."

Devon grew wary as the family quarreled. He didn't seem to be a member of the family anymore. Suddenly he was a guest—a guest with a lot of money. They knew about the will—and his inheritance too. *What's theirs is mine, and what's mine is theirs. . . .*

Devon stabbed at his pie crust, pushing away his discomfort. His relatives were warm and loving and open. They had welcomed him with open arms. They were just doing a little wishing, like everyone else did. It was completely harmless.

Chapter 5

"I can't believe Fowler Crest burned down!" Amy Sutton exclaimed on Monday at noon in the Sweet Valley High cafeteria, her slate gray eyes wide with concern.

"It is absolutely *unbelievable*," Maria Santelli agreed, shaking her head. "Who would have ever imagined that Lila's beautiful mansion would go up in flames?"

Jessica sighed, biting into her turkey sandwich worriedly. News of the fire had been splashed all over the newspapers that morning, and it was all everybody had been talking about in school the entire day. Apparently the Fowler Crest fire was the worst to hit Sweet Valley in years.

Jessica frowned. Lila wouldn't be pleased when she found out that she was the talk of the town—at least not for such a horrible reason. Plus somehow the information had leaked out that the fire had been the result of arson, and the newspapers had reported that as well.

"Poor Lila," Winston Egbert said sympathetically. "She's been through a lot this weekend." Affectionately known as the class clown, Winston had a reputation for joking about everything. But now his expression was completely serious. Shaking his head in disbelief, he dipped a roll into a bowl of steaming tomato soup and bit into it.

"She must have been terrified," Maria chimed in, leaning over to wipe a few crumbs off Winston's chin. A dynamic and outgoing girl, Maria was a member of the cheerleading squad and the student council. She and Winston had been a couple for a long time.

Amy puffed out her cheeks, blowing a wisp of blond hair out of her face. "I just wish I'd been here," she said. "How is Lila doing?"

Jessica shrugged. "She's OK," she said. "She suffered severe smoke inhalation, but otherwise she's fine."

Bruce Patman's eyes narrowed. "Are you sure there's not more to the story?" he asked suspiciously.

Jessica eyed him in disgust. Clearly Bruce was hoping to get some dirt on Lila, whom he considered to be his greatest rival. As the richest families in town, the Patmans and the Fowlers had been feuding for years. Henry Wilson Patman was a canning industry mogul who came from old money, and he resented George Fowler's newer success in the computer chip business.

"Yeah, I heard that her hair caught on fire," Winston put in, a worried look on his face. He picked up an orange and began peeling it, throwing the rinds on his tray.

Jessica gritted her teeth. She couldn't believe the outrageous rumors that had been spreading like wildfire along the Sweet Valley High grapevine. Complete strangers had been grabbing her in the hall for information. "Is it true that Lila Fowler suffered third-degree burns?" a freshman girl had asked her. "Will Lila be permanently scarred?" a sophomore boy had inquired. "I heard Lila's at a private spa in L.A., having her face reconstructed," someone else had said.

"That's not what I heard," Bruce asserted. "I heard that her dress caught on fire and that she ran out of the house completely aflame." He stabbed at a couple of french fries with his fork.

Maria looked at him quickly. "That's a horrible thing to say!" she exclaimed, her hazel eyes crinkled in distaste.

Bruce shrugged. "Just reporting what I heard." He stuffed a forkful of fries in his mouth.

Jessica held up a hand. "OK, let's get one thing straight. I have seen Lila with my own eyes. She's at Fowler Memorial Hospital, and she's perfectly fine—no burns, no surgery, no reconstruction."

Amy exhaled sharply. "Well, that's all that counts," she said, looking visibly relieved. "Maybe we should all go pay her a visit after school."

Jessica shook her head quickly. "I don't think Lila's really in the mood to see people right now," she said. "Besides, she's coming home today." She crumpled up the plastic wrap from her sandwich and stuffed it in her brown paper bag.

"Home," Amy repeated. "She doesn't really have a home anymore." Amy cupped her bowl of soup as if to warm her hands. "According to the papers, the house was entirely razed to the ground."

Bruce snickered. "It's a real shame that the beautiful Fowler mansion is no more," he put in snidely. He picked up his hamburger and took a big bite.

Jessica shot him an angry look. "For your information, just one wing burned down," she said huffily. "And it will be even nicer than it was after they redecorate."

"I don't think the issue is the house," Winston put in. "It's *who* would have done such a thing."

"And *why*," Maria added.

Amy rested her chin on her hands. "Maybe it was just a random act of violence," she suggested. "Maybe some nut just suddenly freaked out and went on a burning spree."

"I doubt it," Winston said. "It sounds to me more like a deliberate act of violence. After all, Fowler Crest isn't exactly easily accessible.

73

Whoever started the fire made a decision in advance to go to the estate." He leaned over and took a chocolate chip cookie from Maria's tray.

Maria nodded. "I agree with Winston." She bit her lip thoughtfully. "Maybe it was one of George Fowler's business acquaintances."

"Or an employee who he fired sometime," Winston put in, taking a bite of the cookie.

"Oh, what's the point of surmising?" Bruce interrupted, cutting the conversation short. "It could have been one of a million people. George Fowler has a lot of enemies."

Jessica opened her mouth to retort, but then she shut it again, sighing. Unfortunately Bruce was right. When it came to business, George Fowler could be ruthless. And a lot of people begrudged him his power and position.

"What if they weren't after Mr. Fowler at all?" Amy wondered, her eyes narrowed.

"What do you mean?" Jessica asked, looking at her quickly.

Amy looked worried. "Maybe they were after Lila."

"But who would want to hurt Lila?" Jessica asked.

Amy shrugged. "I don't know. But there are a lot of jealous people in this town."

Jessica's stomach knotted in fear. Amy was right. A lot of kids envied Lila for her status and her looks. Maybe the arsonist was right here at

Sweet Valley High. Maybe it was somebody they knew.

Jessica glanced around at the students in the cafeteria, feeling suddenly chilled.

"The freedom train is here!" Jessica exclaimed, peeking her head into Lila's hospital room on Monday afternoon after school.

Lila was sitting in a chair in the corner, staring out the window. She was fully dressed, and her bags were packed and sitting by her side. She was wearing a casual black cotton dress and a pair of flat black pumps that Jessica had loaned her.

Lila turned at the sound of Jessica's voice, giving her a small smile. Lila looked better than she had in days. Her hair was freshly washed and hung in loose waves over her shoulders, and her cheeks had regained some color.

"You ready to go?" Jessica asked.

"I've been ready for the last three hours," Lila said, standing up quickly. She picked up her bag and slung it over her shoulder. Then she headed across the room and took Jessica's arm, leading her out the door. "I feel like I've been here forever."

The girls walked rapidly down the hall to the elevator bank. "I just want to get out of here and never come back," Lila said as they took the elevator down to the first floor. "I've never seen so much white in my life."

"It is a bit one-dimensional," Jessica agreed.

"My mother could give the hospital staff a few interior design tips."

The elevator reached the first floor, and the girls stepped out into a throng of waiting nurses. They steered their way around the staff and headed down the long white hall.

"Do you have to check out or anything?" Jessica asked as they passed the front desk.

Lila shook her head. "Nope, I signed all the papers this afternoon," she said. "I got a perfect bill of health and am now as free as a bird."

Lila pushed through the glass doors of the lobby, and Jessica quickly followed.

"What a relief!" Lila exclaimed, taking great gulps of fresh air. "I thought I'd never get out of there." Then she glanced around the parking lot. "Where's the freedom train?"

Jessica pointed to the twins' Jeep, and the girls headed toward it.

A few minutes later they were on the road. The sun was beginning to set, and the late afternoon rays cast a slanting glare on the road. Jessica fished in the bag by her side for her sunglasses.

Lila flicked on the radio and fiddled with the knob. "So, how was school today?" she asked, stopping at a popular rock station.

"Well, Mom, it was just fine," Jessica responded, putting on her sunglasses. She slowed down and turned onto the two-lane highway, which was packed with rush hour traffic.

"I suppose I was the big news," Lila said.

Jessica grimaced as she maneuvered the Jeep into the left lane. "Sort of," she admitted. "You seem to be the topic of the moment."

Lila sighed. "I know," she said. "I bought the newspapers today at the newsstand in the hospital." She reached for the overnight bag Jessica had supplied for her and unzipped it, pulling out a stack of papers. "Look at these headlines," she said, slapping a paper with her hand. "'Fowler Crest a Raging Inferno!' and 'Wild Arsonist on the Loose!'"

Jessica glanced over at the papers in Lila's hand. "Well, those are just tabloids," she said, turning her attention back to the road. The cars were moving at a slow crawl. Jessica shifted into low gear, tapping her foot impatiently on the pedal.

"But look at *Sweet Valley News*," Lila said, holding it up and pointing to the headline. "It's no better. 'Biggest Fire to Hit Sweet Valley in Decades.'"

Jessica nodded. "Yeah, you're right," she said. "It's all a bit sensationalistic."

Lila heaved a sigh. "And the worst of it is that everybody knows the fire was arson now," she said. "The entire school is going to be looking at me like I'm some weirdo being stalked." Lila slumped down in her seat dejectedly. "It's like the John Pfeifer nightmare all over again."

Jessica flicked on her turn signal and moved

into the right lane. "I'm sure it will all blow over in a few days," she said reassuringly.

Lila rubbed her forehead. "I hope so," she said, inching down farther in her seat and drawing her knees up to rest them on the dashboard. "Do you think I have to go back to school tomorrow?"

Jessica shook her head, waving her right hand in the air. "Nah, I'm sure you can get a few days out of this," she said. "You know, emotional trauma and all that."

Lila nodded and fell silent.

Jessica took the exit ramp and coasted onto Valley Crest Road, relieved to be out of the congestion of the highway. She put her foot on the accelerator and headed toward Lila's house. The traffic was moving faster in town, and they reached Lila's area in a few minutes.

Jessica's stomach tightened nervously as they approached Fowler Crest. She wished for the thousandth time that Lila would go home with her.

"Home, sweet home," Lila said, twirling an index finger in the air.

Jessica glanced over at her best friend nervously. Lila was sitting up in her seat, and her face was set, as if she was expecting the worst.

Jessica drove through the wrought iron front gate, surprised to see the lush grounds still intact. The sculptured lawns stretched out on either side of the long driveway, and the fountain sparkled in the late afternoon sun.

Jessica turned onto the circular drive in front of the estate and pulled to a stop. Both girls sucked in their breath.

"Omigosh," Lila said, clapping her hand over her mouth.

Jessica stared at the mansion in dismay.

One side of the stone structure was completely crushed. It looked like the roof had caved in. The entire facade of the west wing was blackened, and the windows were all gone, creating the bizarre impression that the mansion was gaping at them. The rest of the house was a dusty gray, and piles of rubble covered the ground. Thick orange police tape was tied around the front banister, and a Proceed with Caution sign stood on the front lawn.

Jessica was stunned by the extent of the damage. Even though she had known that the west wing had burned down, she hadn't really visualized what that meant. She hadn't realized that the house itself would actually be destroyed.

Jessica bit her lip, looking over at Lila in concern.

Lila was just gazing at the mansion in shock. Her face was ashen, and her eyes were spilling over with tears. But when she felt Jessica's eyes on her, she clenched her jaw and blinked a few times, clearly trying to compose herself.

Lila wiped at her cheeks with the back of her hand and took a deep breath. "OK, let's get this over with," she said, grabbing hold of the door handle.

"Lila, are you sure you can deal with this?" Jessica asked as they got out of the car.

Lila nodded, heading up the walk determinedly. Jessica slammed the door shut and hurried after her.

But Lila stopped short as they reached the top step. The front door was entirely gone. "Well, I guess I won't be needing my keys," she said dryly. She and Jessica stepped into the doorway cautiously.

The marble foyer was still intact. The only signs of damage seemed to be smoke induced. The long hanging mirror was blackened, and the marble sconce was covered with a layer of debris. Huge puddles of water covered the floor, with shards of glass floating in them.

"Huh!" Lila exclaimed, sucking in her breath. Her mouth dropped open, and she pointed to the ceiling. Jessica followed her gaze, and her eyes widened. The crystal chandelier was gone. Apparently it had crashed to the floor and splintered into pieces.

"That . . . that was an antique chandelier," Lila breathed. "It's been in my family for ages. My mother's going to have a fit."

"No, she won't," Jessica said, shaking her head firmly. "Remember, everything's insured. Your mother will just be happy that you're alive."

"First she'll be happy I'm alive," Lila corrected her. "Then she'll kill me."

"Try not to think about it," Jessica said. "It's not like the fire was your fault."

Lila nodded distractedly as the girls walked carefully around the pieces of glass and headed down the hall to check out the rest of the damage.

"Oh, boy," Lila muttered under her breath as they entered the living room. The elegant salon had been reduced to a dusty pile of rubble, and everything had been hosed down. Water still dripped down the walls, and the floorboards were dark and damp. The room exuded a pungent odor of dampened wood and wet ashes.

Jessica had the strange impression of being in the skeleton of a room. All that remained of the velvet furniture were bony wooden frames, and wispy bits of curtains hung off the iron rods, flapping eerily in the empty window frames. The only thing left in the room was the fireplace, which was covered in a thick layer of black soot.

Jessica put a comforting arm around her friend. But Lila was just staring across the room, her eyes wide. "That could have been me," she whispered, pointing to the skeleton of the divan. Her eyes welled up with tears again.

"But it wasn't," Jessica said, squeezing her shoulders. "You were very, very lucky."

Lila heaved a deep sigh. "Yes, I was," she said quietly, as if she had just realized it for the first time.

The girls walked through the rest of the house,

taking inventory. Almost all the furniture in the west wing had been destroyed. The only standing pieces were the grand piano and the glass dining-room table. Except for a few remaining antique pieces scattered among the debris, almost all the artwork was ruined as well.

The east wing was in pretty bad shape too. Even though the fire hadn't reached it, the rooms had suffered severe smoke damage. All the furniture was blackened, and a thin layer of ashes covered the floor. Even the moldings on the wall and the paintings were covered with a wet, black film.

Lila shook her head as they headed back to the west wing. "We might as well just raze the house to the ground entirely," she remarked. She stopped in the middle of the ballroom, taking in the damage with an expression of disbelief on her face.

"Do you want me to help you move all the salvageable stuff into the east wing?" Jessica offered.

Lila shook her head. "The police told me not to touch anything," she said. "The D.A. himself paid me a visit in the hospital today."

Jessica was silent. Obviously they wanted to find clues leading to the arsonist. She looked around the dusty ruins of the enormous room, feeling suddenly spooked. "Lila, let's get out of here," she said quickly. "Why don't we go to the Dairi Burger and grab a shake?"

Lila rubbed her neck. "I'm not really up for it,"

she said. "I'm pretty tired. I think I'm going to turn in for the night."

"You really should come home with me," Jessica said. "After all, there *is* an arsonist on the loose." She wiped off the front of her T-shirt, which was covered with dust.

But Lila shook her head. "No, I want to stay here," she answered, her voice just a whisper. "It's all I've got left."

"But Li, you don't even have a bed to sleep in," Jessica protested, rubbing her hands together to get the dust off them. "The police said all the bedrooms have been severely damaged."

Lila shrugged. "I can sleep in the pool house."

"Then I'll stay with you in the pool house," Jessica offered quickly.

"Jess, I really appreciate the offer, but I'd prefer to be alone," Lila insisted.

Jessica searched her friend's face. Lila looked tired and drained, but her eyes had a defiant expression in them. Clearly she wasn't going to change her mind.

"OK," Jessica agreed finally. "But don't think I like it."

She turned reluctantly and headed for the doorway. But before she crossed the threshold, she took one look back. Lila was standing perfectly still, staring at the remains. Her shoulder blades stood out in Jessica's thin dress, making her seem frail and vulnerable.

Jessica shivered. She knew Lila was in danger. She could feel it in her bones. She just didn't know what she could do to protect her.

After Jessica left, Lila wandered through the rooms of the ghost house, feeling particularly nostalgic. She stood in the center of the living room, thinking back to the previous Christmas. Her father had set up a huge pine tree next to the fireplace, and her mother had baked a special French cake called a *bûche de Noël*. They had opened their gifts together in front of the fire. It had been Lila's first Christmas with her whole family together.

Then she headed for the ballroom, remembering her sixteenth birthday. She'd thrown a huge bash for all her friends, with a live band and caterers. Almost everybody in the junior class had shown up for the event, and they'd danced for hours.

Finally she climbed up the steps leading to her bedroom, a tight knot of anxiety in her stomach. She knew the fire had reached the second floor, but she had been told that the damage was less severe. She couldn't help retaining the tiny hope that all her personal stuff hadn't been destroyed.

Lila coughed as she reached the top of the staircase. The walls were charred and frayed, and a thick layer of dust seemed to hang in the air. As she walked down the hall the stiff carpet crunched underneath her feet.

Lila pushed open her bedroom door cautiously. Her furniture was still standing, but it was charred and covered with thick black soot. Lila touched the four-poster bed, then the antique bureau. Everything was damp from the firefighters' hoses. It would all have to be replaced.

Lila's eyes widened as she took in her jewelry box on the top of the bureau. Her jewelry appeared to have melted into one thick clump. She reached out a hand and fingered what used to be her necklaces. Now they were just a blackened mass of gold. Her chest tight, she pulled open a little drawer that held her antique rings. The gems were cracked, and they had melted together as well, forming a tiny ruby and emerald puddle.

Lila took a step back, feeling stung. Her mother had given her the ruby ring for her sixteenth birthday, and the emerald had been in her family for generations. The jewelry could be replaced, but the sentiments attached to them couldn't be. Nothing could ever take the place of her family heirlooms.

Feeling dispirited, Lila went to the walk-in closet and pulled open a door. She sucked in her breath at the sight that greeted her. Her entire wardrobe seemed to have disappeared into nothing. Frayed remains of clothing hung on hangers, and thick piles of ashes covered the floor. Lila reached out to finger a long red silk dress that was still hanging. It disintegrated at her touch, joining the ashes on the floor. Lila jumped back, blinking back tears.

Lila squeezed her eyes shut and took a deep breath. *It's just clothing,* she told herself firmly. *Clothes don't matter. They can be replaced.*

Standing up on her tiptoes, she reached for two precious metal boxes stacked up on the shelf. As she pulled them down, a cloud of soot rose in the air. Lila coughed and waved the dust away. When the smoke cleared, she examined the ornate boxes in her hand. They appeared to be undamaged. Lila closed her eyes, breathing a sigh of relief.

Lila sat down on the floor, the two boxes in her lap. They held all her pictures and souvenirs from her trips since childhood. Taking a deep breath, she unclasped the golden latch of one of the boxes and lifted the lid. Hot tears sprang to her eyes. Everything was charred and soaking. She pulled out a brochure from the French Riviera. It hung limply in her hand.

Sighing, Lila pushed aside the box and turned to the other one. Sure enough, her pictures were soaked as well. They stuck together in clumps, with thick black streaks across the surfaces. Lila unglued a smudged photo of herself and Jessica and held it up in the air. They were on the beach with their arms around each other, smiling as if they didn't have a care in the world. Lila threw the picture away in disgust.

Her heart heavy, Lila stood up and went to the

desk. Kneeling down, she reached into the bottom drawer and pulled out a cardboard box. This was the most important item of all. It contained all the letters she had ever received in her life.

Lila sat back on her heels and rested the box on her knees. Her hands shaking, she carefully lifted the lid. Her letters were a uniform, soggy mass. They were damp and worn, and the pages were charred at the edges. Lila lifted out the top envelope and held it up. The ink was smeared so badly that she could no longer make out the writing.

Lila felt a fierce dart of pain shoot through her. This was something that could never, ever be replaced. And to think she had actually destroyed Bo's letters on her own. Lila dropped her head in her hands. *This is what you get for not appreciating what you have,* she berated herself.

Lila leaned against the bed, drawing her knees up to her chest and wrapping her arms around them. It was worse than she'd expected. She had been sure that some of her stuff would have survived.

Lila sighed deeply. The material things didn't really have any meaning—they could all be replaced. But her pictures and letters and souvenirs from trips had all disappeared as well, and there was no way to bring them back.

Lila didn't know if she'd ever felt this horrible in her life. She felt even worse than she did after that awful incident with John Pfeifer that had left her so fragile.

Lila closed her eyes, thinking back to the traumatic experience. She had gone out on a date with John Pfeifer, and he had lunged at her in the car, ripping her clothes as he attacked her. She had managed to fight him off and get away, but she had been traumatized for months. After that experience she had no longer trusted guys and had no interest in dating. She had only begun to heal after a long round of therapy sessions.

Lila pushed at a pile of rubble with her foot, feeling like she'd hit rock bottom. Compared to this, the incident with John Pfeifer was nothing. She had been badly scarred, but she had been able to heal. There was no way she could bring back her memories. It was like her whole life had been burned away in a matter of minutes.

A tear came to her eye and trickled slowly down her cheek.

Chapter 6

Steven steered his Volkswagen quickly along the winding roads of Sweet Valley early Monday evening. He was on his way to Fowler Crest to pay Lila a visit. He was eager to get to the bottom of the case, and Lila was a key suspect. Steven was determined to figure out if she might have had any motivation to set the mansion on fire.

Steven turned onto Valley Crest Road, thinking back to what Jessica had told him about her best friend. Apparently Lila had grown up like a typical rich kid—spoiled, privileged, and alone. Her parents had been virtually absent. Her mother had been living in France for most of Lila's childhood, and her father spent most of his time traveling on business. Obviously Lila had been forced to grow up quickly.

Steven slowed down the car as he approached an intersection, thinking hard. Lila had been Jessica's best friend for years, and she often hung out at the Wakefield house. She had always appeared together and well-adjusted to Steven, but now he had a feeling that was just a facade. After all, a childhood of solitude must leave its mark. And Jessica had hinted at a trauma in Lila's past as well.

A car honked and Steven slammed on the brakes, realizing that he had been about to go through a red light. He drummed his fingers on the steering wheel, waiting impatiently at the intersection. Not only did he want to talk to Lila about the case, but he wanted to make sure she was OK. Jessica had rushed into the house that evening in a state of panic. She was terrified about Lila staying alone. She had practically begged Steven to get a police order forbidding her to stay in the house. But unfortunately that was against the law.

The light turned green, and Steven stepped on the accelerator. *Jessica is right to be worried,* he thought. It was crazy for Lila to be alone. It was very possible that she was in serious danger. Plus she had no way of contacting the outside world. He had tried to call her to set up an appointment, but apparently the phone lines had been severed in the fire.

Steven reached Fowler Crest and cut his speed. As he drove up the winding driveway he sucked in his breath. "Pretty impressive," he whispered to himself. The mansion looked like it had been crushed on one end. Whoever had set the fire had done a thorough job.

Steven hopped out of his car and headed up the

front walk. He instinctively put his hand up to knock on the front door, but then he blinked. The door was completely gone. He peeked his head into the foyer. "Hello? Anybody here?" he called out.

There was no response, so Steven stepped over the threshold. The marble foyer was still in good shape, but a thick layer of black soot lined everything, and the floor was slippery from the firefighters' hoses. "Lila?" he called out. "It's Steven Wakefield." There was no answer.

Steven walked through the west wing, taking mental notes. It appeared to be entirely demolished. Only the bare frame of some furniture remained. The rooms most badly hit were the den, the dining room, and the study—the three rooms that surrounded the living room. Unlike the other chambers, virtually nothing remained in them. Even the artwork and accessories had been destroyed. Steven paused in the den, narrowing his eyes in thought. The fire must have started in those rooms.

"Lila?" Steven called out again. His voice echoed strangely in the shadow of a house. Suddenly Steven began to get nervous, and Jessica's words came back to him. *I'm worried about her, Steven,* she had said that evening. *I've got a weird feeling about this.* What if Jessica was right? What if something had happened to Lila? What if the arsonist was around right now?

Steven pushed through the back door and hurried out onto the patio, wondering if Lila had gone outside. The back patio stood in stark relief to the devastated interior of the house. It was lovely and bright, with red clay tiles and hanging baskets of plants. Tall lemon trees lined the tiles, and an Olympic-size pool sparkled quietly in the moonlight.

Steven chewed on his lower lip, feeling more and more concerned. He couldn't imagine where Lila could be. Then he spotted a light coming from the pool house. A shadowy female figure was carrying something through the door.

Steven let out his breath. Then he stood still for a moment to compose himself. He couldn't let Lila see how worried he was. He wanted to reassure her, not scare her.

Forcing himself to walk at a normal pace, Steven headed across the patio. "Hi, Lila!" he called out casually.

Lila turned quickly at the sound of his voice. "Oh, hi, Steven," she said. She held a stack of boxes in her arms. Then she frowned, clearly confused. "What are you doing here?" she asked.

Steven shrugged as he reached her. "I just wanted to see how you were," he explained. "Jessica was worried about you." He didn't want to tell her he'd been put on the case yet. For now he wanted to build up her confidence in him.

Lila nodded. "Oh," she said. But she didn't look particularly thrilled to have company.

"So, are you getting ready for the whirlwind

shopping spree my sister has planned?" Steven asked, his voice light.

Lila's serious expression was sobering. "I know Jessica is trying to make me feel better, but *shopping?* When my whole life has been destroyed?" she asked, an expression of disbelief on her face. "I could never replace the things I've lost—and all the memories attached to them."

Steven immediately regretted his words. Obviously Lila wasn't in the mood for light bantering. And she wasn't ready to be cheered up. She probably just needed somebody to talk to—and some time to heal.

"Can I help you with that?" Steven asked, holding open the door for her.

Lila shook her head. "No, thanks, I'm OK," she said, ducking under his arm. Steven followed her into the pool house and shut the door behind them.

Lila set the boxes carefully on a table and walked over to the bureau, where she began to arrange a few personal items. She had put together a makeshift home. A cot was set up against the wall, and a small table covered with a bright yellow tablecloth was nestled in the corner. Lila had also moved a few potted plants into the pool house and had lined the windows with flowers. The small wooden room was actually quite cozy.

Steven sat down on a chair at the tiny square table in the corner, watching her in surprise. He had always thought of Jessica's best friend as a ditz with a credit card. He would have expected her to moan and complain in a crisis like this, but instead she was acting very strong and self-sufficient.

Lila really has a lot of fight in her, Steven thought. Her whole life had just been destroyed, and she was already setting up a new one. She was handling this with a lot of courage and dignity.

But when she went to pick up one of the small metal boxes, he could see her expression change. Her jaw tightened, and tears came to her eyes. She sat down on the bed with the box on her lap.

"Hey, what's wrong?" Steven asked, standing up and joining her on the cot.

"It's just that . . . that *everything* was destroyed," Lila explained, waving a distraught hand in the air. "These boxes contain my whole life—all my pictures and souvenirs," she said. She opened the lid to reveal a cluster of wet photos stuck together. "They were all ruined."

Steven fingered one of the pictures. "That's really tough, Lila," he said quietly.

Lila stood up and began pacing the room. "Every minute I think of something else that was lost," she said.

Steven was silent, listening to her.

"The ancient Chinese fan that my mother gave me for my sixteenth birthday, the silk sari that I got from a Hindu priest in India, the emerald ring that belonged to my great-grandmother." Lila waved a hand in the air. "It's like each thing was attached to a specific place and time. And with the loss of the thing, I feel like I've lost the experience as well."

Steven was surprised at the depth of Lila's emotions and the wisdom in her words. Even though the items she described constituted a luxury that was beyond anything Steven had experienced, the memories she shared carried real emotions. He began to see the person behind the shallow image he'd always had of her.

Could this really be a person who would set fire to her own home? he wondered. *Is this all a brilliant acting job?* He just couldn't believe it.

Lila sighed, sounding older than her age. "You know, it's funny. They're just things, but they're our memories as well. When you see a picture or a keepsake, a whole world comes back to you, and times you had forgotten return to you as well." Lila leaned against the wall, looking deeply pained. "I've lost all of that now," she whispered.

Steven couldn't think of anything to say. Unfortunately Lila was right. Her souvenirs and pictures really did matter. They represented her entire past. She had lost some invaluable memories.

Lila knelt down by the bed, placing the box carefully on the trunk in front of it. "I just couldn't bear to give up the stuff yet," she said. "I know it's silly, but I'd rather have ruined pictures than no pictures at all."

"I don't blame you for being upset about losing all your souvenirs," Steven said, his voice rough.

"The things don't matter, but your memories do."

Lila gave him a small smile, obviously grateful for the support.

"I know how devastating this is," Steven continued, "but you should be thankful for what you *do* have—your life, your friends, your family—the things that really count." Steven stood up. "After all, you could have been killed in the fire."

Lila nodded. "Yeah, you're right," she said softly.

Then she sat back on her heels, her expression downcast again. "But the nightmare's not over yet," she said in a tiny voice. "I'm in danger once again." Lila heaved a deep sigh. "It's like the whole John Pfeifer story all over again."

Steven's ears perked up at the name. He took a seat on a low stool across from her and caught her eyes. "The John Pfeifer story?" he inquired.

"Oh, it's nothing," Lila said, her face flushing. She quickly averted her gaze.

Steven didn't press the issue, remembering his conversation with his sisters about how personal whatever had happened between Lila and this Pfeifer person had been. But he filed away the information. Obviously this guy had seriously traumatized her. Maybe it had something to do with the case. *But what?* Steven wondered. Well, he decided, he would just have to be patient. If he built up Lila's trust, maybe she would confide in him eventually.

Lila sank down on the edge of the cot, looking dejected. "Whoever tried to burn down the house didn't succeed, at least not totally," she said, her lips quivering slightly. "And now they might come back."

"Well, don't worry about that," Steven said firmly, taking a seat next to her. "We're going to find them."

Lila blinked and looked up at him. "We?" she questioned.

"I'm working at the D.A.'s office, and I've been assigned to investigate the case," Steven explained. "So I'll be with you every step of the way."

Lila's eyes welled up with grateful tears. "Oh, I'm so happy you've been sent to help me," she said. She smiled up at him through her tears, and Steven felt his heart go out to her. "I was feeling so angry—and scared—and alone."

"Well, you're not alone anymore," Steven said, wrapping a comforting arm around her shoulders.

Lila rested her head against his chest and snuggled up against him. "Steven, please find out who did this," she whispered.

"Don't worry, I will," Steven told her reassuringly. He tightened his hold slightly and vowed to make his words come true. Lila was so young and vulnerable. He couldn't help wanting to protect her.

"So this was where I was when the fire started," Lila said, pointing to the brick fireplace in the living room. "I had lit a fire and was sitting in front of it."

Lila felt better than she had all day. At first she had been irritated that Jessica's brother had just appeared at her home uninvited, but now she was glad he had shown up. And she was thrilled that he was investigating the case. It was as if her white knight had ridden up with a promise to find the fire-breathing dragon. She had been feeling completely raw and vulnerable back in the pool house, but Steven's soothing presence was taking away all her fears.

"And what were you doing before the fire started?" Steven asked.

Lila hesitated. She didn't really want to tell Steven about Bo and burning his letters. It was still so painful. And the point of destroying the mementos was to put her relationship with Bo behind her. Not to dredge it up again.

"Nothing, really," Lila said, leaning against the wall. Then she quickly jumped away, realizing she had just covered her arm in soot. Lila quickly wiped off her sleeve, coughing as dust filled the air.

Steven shook his head. "Lila, if we're going to crack this case, I've got to know exactly what you were doing and what you were thinking when the fire began," he said, his voice strong.

Lila nodded, but she didn't say anything. She felt strangely vulnerable, as if her whole life were being exposed.

"The police report indicated that you'd been

lighting matches before the fire," Steven said in a gentle voice.

"But what does that have to do with it?" Lila asked, feeling confused.

Steven just looked at her, and suddenly the relevance of his words hit her with brute force. They thought she had set the fire! Lila felt a wave of shock rock her entire body. "But . . . but you can't possibly think I'm responsible!" she protested.

Steven shook his head firmly. "Of course not," he said softly. "I'm on your side, Lila. But if we're going to get at the truth, we've got to be a team. I need to know everything. Everything, if I'm going to crack this case."

Lila sighed deeply. "OK. Well, I was sitting in front of the fireplace." She walked over to the remains of the Persian rug in front of the hearth and knelt down to demonstrate. Steven dusted off the rug and sat down next to her to listen.

Lila took a deep breath. "I . . . I was going out with this guy named Bo who I met at camp, and we . . . we had just broken up. I was upset."

She glanced at Steven from under her eyelids, feeling silly for recounting the details of her personal life. But Steven was looking at her with sympathy in his eyes, and he was nodding as if he understood.

Lila ran a finger through her hair. "So finally I decided I had to get rid of all memories of him—"

"And to burn all his letters," Steven finished for her.

Lila glanced at him in surprise. "How did you know that?"

Steven grinned. "I've been there before."

Lila felt herself really relaxing. It actually felt good to talk about Bo to somebody who understood. She sat down and drew her knees up to her chest. "So I threw the letters in the fire, and then I fell asleep on the divan."

"Which was—?" Steven asked.

"Which was here," Lila said, pointing to the space behind her. "I don't know how much time passed, but when I woke up, flames were rushing into the room," she finished. "I wanted to get out the window, but suddenly everything was catching fire. I guess I must have passed out."

"So the flames came from that direction," Steven said, indicating the entranceway.

"From the door," Lila affirmed.

Steven nodded, clearly digesting the information. His eyes got a faraway look in them, and he stared off into space. "You know, it's funny," he remarked quietly. "After Billie and I broke up, I felt like my whole life had gone up in flames." Then he grinned at her. "But of course, my situation was just metaphorical."

Lila's eyes widened. "You and Billie broke up?"

Steven nodded, a hint of pain in his deep brown eyes.

"What happened?" Lila asked.

Steven hesitated, but then he began to tell her

the story. "Well, it all started when I found out I got the internship at the D.A.'s office," he said.

As Steven talked about Billie, Lila found herself studying him. It was as if she were seeing him for the first time. He was tall and dark like his father, with a strong jaw and beautiful, deep brown eyes that shone with a luminous light when he spoke.

Lila silently wondered why she had never noticed how handsome Steven was before.

Chapter 7

Lila is sitting in front of a fire, mesmerized by the dancing red lights. One by one she throws her love letters into the hearth, watching in fascination as the flickering flames catch the edges of the pages and devour them.

Then the letters are gone, and Lila is all alone.

The flames crackle hungrily. "Poor little rich girl, poor little rich girl," their words echo in the room.

Suddenly the fire is all around her. The room is full of thick, black smoke. The flames lick at her feet. But Lila can't move. She is rooted to the spot.

"Poor little rich girl, poor little rich girl," sing the mocking flames.

The words get louder and louder as the flames dance around her. The fire is getting higher and higher, and the red heat is getting closer and closer to her body. Lila opens her mouth to scream, but no sound comes out.

Lila moaned and backed up against the wall, trying to get away from the flames. "No, no!" she whimpered out loud. "Please, no!"

Lila woke up with a start, her heart pounding in her chest. She found herself pressed up against the wall with the covers tangled around her. She was in a cold sweat, and her whole body was trembling.

She glanced around the room, trying to get her bearings. She was in a small, dark shed, and strange shadows were crawling on the walls. Why was it so cold? Where was the fire? And where was *she*?

Lila blinked, trying to clear her mind. Then the events of the past few days came back to her—the fire, the hospital, her demolished home. It was Tuesday morning, and she was out in the pool house.

Lila shuddered in relief as she realized she had just been dreaming. She untangled the covers and sat up in bed, wrapping her arms around her knees. The disturbing images of her dream resonated in her mind. She saw the flickering red flames and the thick black smoke. She heard the mocking voice of the fire.

Suddenly Lila recalled the darting snakes' tongues weaving their way toward her on Friday night. She remembered staring at them, mesmerized, before she passed out.

A deep tremor surged through her body. What if the firefighters had come one moment later? What if the fire had reached *her?*

Lila pulled the covers around her shoulders. *But it didn't,* she reassured herself. *You're fine. And you're going to be fine.*

Lila shook her head hard, as if she could physically shake the upsetting images from her mind. Leaning over, she picked up her alarm clock and squinted at it. It was only six A.M.

It was cool and dark and strangely quiet out in the pool house. Lila could hear the sounds of the wind rustling in the trees and the water sloshing softly against the sides of the pool. It was as if she were enclosed in some desolate, isolated universe. She felt completely and utterly alone.

Lila got back in bed and pulled her covers over her, wrapping them tightly around her body. But she couldn't go back to sleep. She lay flat on her back and stared at the wooden beams on the ceiling, haunted by the flickering flames that had mocked her in her dream.

Steven sat at his desk at the D.A.'s office on Tuesday afternoon, deep in thought. He had been given a small cubicle in the corner, which was separated from the other employees by a standing orange divider. His desk came equipped with a computer and a portable printer, as well as thick pads of yellow memo paper and an in box.

Steven had spent the morning writing up a report on the Fowler Crest fire. He had tried to recreate the event based on his observations of the damage and the information that he had garnered from Lila the day before. According to his analysis, the fire had started in three rooms almost simultaneously: the den, the dining room, and the study. Those rooms were well separated, which reconfirmed the fact that the fire was an act of arson.

Steven leaned back in his chair, studying the rough diagram of the west wing that he had sketched on a piece of memo paper. The three rooms formed a triangular pattern around the living room, which indicated that the room in which Lila had fallen asleep had been the ultimate goal. Steven sighed. It appeared that the arsonist's main target wasn't the Fowler Crest mansion but Lila herself.

Joe Garrison was right on the mark when he decided to concentrate on Lila, Steven thought. But not because Lila was guilty—because she was in danger. Steven picked up his profile of Lila, glancing through what he had written. *Lila Fowler: sixteen-year-old daughter of George and Grace Fowler; emotionally stable and intellectually mature; frightened and shaken up in the aftermath of the fire but strong, proud, and independent.*

Steven let the paper drift onto the desk, thinking of how sad and scared Lila had seemed the night before. It had been almost impossible to leave her. She had an irresistible combination of strength and vulnerability. The more he got to know her, the more Steven respected her—and the more he wanted to protect her.

Steven tapped the eraser end of his pencil on his desk. Now he had two goals: He wanted to find the arsonist, and he wanted to clear Lila's name. After visiting with her the night before, he was sure she was innocent. All the facts of the case supported it.

Just then Joe Garrison popped his head into the cubicle. "Steven, see me in my office," he demanded, his voice gruff as usual.

"Sure," Steven responded, standing up quickly. He stacked up his papers and threw them in a file. Then he followed his boss across the room to his office.

"So what do you have?" Mr. Garrison asked Steven as soon as he was in the door. The D.A. took a seat behind his desk, and Steven sat down across from him.

"Well, I mapped out the course of the fire and wrote up a report of the events," Steven reported. He spread out a sheet of paper on the desk, where he had drawn a layout of the west wing. "Based on the extent of the damage and the concentration of smoke traces, I think the first fire must have started here, in the dining room." Steven pointed to a big red X. "The fire then traveled through the foyer to the living room."

"The first fire?" Joe Garrison repeated.

Steven frowned. "Well, apparently the arsonist did a thorough job. I observed that fires were started in three separate places—the dining room, the den, and the study." Steven pointed to two smaller Xs that marked the other areas. "And all three places converge on the living room."

Mr. Garrison picked up the layout and studied it. He nodded slowly, whistling softly. "Nice work, Steven," he said. "This is an invaluable piece of analysis. As soon as renovations begin on the mansion all this evidence will be gone."

Steven sat back in his chair. "There's just one thing that bothers me," he said. "The fire started in a triangular pattern and moved into the center. It's as if the arsonist wanted to get to Lila herself."

"Or maybe she just wanted to detract any signs of guilt from herself," countered the D.A.

Steven shook his head. "I don't think she's guilty."

Mr. Garrison cocked his head. "Then how do you explain the matches that were found in her pocket and the sulfur traces on her fingertips?" he asked, his voice challenging.

"She was just burning some letters in the fireplace," Steven responded. "And the arsonist's work started in the other rooms of the house."

"That doesn't prove anything," Joe Garrison said in a dismissive voice. He leaned back in his chair and tapped his fingers on the armrest.

"Maybe it was her goal to burn down the house without harming herself in the process. And then she found herself cornered."

"I'm not convinced," Steven insisted, holding his ground. He handed his report on Lila to the D.A. "I've written up a psychological profile of Lila. Her main characteristics are pride and strength. She's clearly scared and vulnerable, but she's trying to be brave at the same time," he explained. "The most convincing evidence in her favor is her show of courage. If she were guilty, then she would make a point of appearing scared, not tough."

Mr. Garrison glanced at the report and shrugged. "Unless she's smart," he said. "Really smart." He dropped the page down on the desk.

Steven squinted at his boss. "What makes you so sure she's a prime suspect in the case?" he asked.

Mr. Garrison leaned forward and spoke softly. "We've got a new piece of evidence," he said. "A team of detectives found an empty gas can in Lila's car."

Steven's mouth dropped open in shock. After his meeting with Lila the day before, he had been convinced that she didn't have anything to do with the case. Had Lila pulled the wool over his eyes? Was she guilty after all?

"Lila Fowler may seem innocent, but you have to look deeper," his boss continued. "Don't let yourself be taken in by a pretty face."

Steven nodded and stood up. Clearly the meeting was over. He pulled open the door and stepped out of the office, feeling like a failure. He wasn't making any progress on the case at all. It was the detectives who had come up with cold, hard evidence. All Steven had was his intuition. Mr. Garrison must think he was a total idiot.

As he walked back to his cubicle his boss's words resonated in Steven's mind. Lila *did* have a pretty face. He hadn't been unaware of it when he was with her the night before. Was Lila's charm clouding his judgment? Was he letting his emotions get in the way of his work?

Steven resolved to be more businesslike. He'd never make it as a lawyer if he got personally involved in his cases.

"OK, let's go over what you need," Jessica said as she and Lila rode the escalator to the second floor of Valley Mall on Tuesday afternoon.

"Well, I guess some skirts and blouses and pants and jackets and dresses," Lila responded in a lackluster tone. The girls stepped off the escalator and headed down the hall. Despite the fact that it was the middle of the week, the mall was packed with late afternoon shoppers.

Jessica looked over at Lila quickly, but her best friend's face was impassive. "Was everything destroyed?" she asked.

Lila nodded. "Yep, every last thing."

Jessica flinched. "Your Chanel suit? Your Gucci evening dress? Your Italian sandals—"

"Jessica!" Lila interrupted. "You don't have to rub it in."

Jessica looked down. "Oh, sorry," she said.

"Don't worry about it," Lila said with a light flick of her wrist.

A woman pushing a baby carriage almost bumped into Jessica, and she jumped out of the way. "Who *are* all these people?" Jessica complained. "Why don't they go shopping on Saturday like they're supposed to?"

The girls wove through the crowd and turned the corner, heading for what they considered to be the fashion section of the mall. Their favorite boutiques, Bibi's and Lisette's, were at the far end of the corridor on the second floor.

Jessica whistled under her breath as they walked down the hall. "A whole new wardrobe," she said. "So where should we start first?"

"Oh, it doesn't really matter to me," Lila said, waving a dismissive hand in the air.

Jessica looked at her best friend carefully. She was still wearing the same black cotton minidress that Jessica had loaned her. "Lila, what happened to the rest of the clothes I gave you?" she asked.

Lila shrugged. "I like this dress."

Jessica shook her head. She was obviously going to have to take charge here. At the moment this girl needed some serious fashion counseling.

Before the fire Lila would have thrown a fit if she had had to wear the same outfit two days in a row. Now she was perfectly content to wear the same clothes every single day.

"Well, why don't we get the basics first—a couple pairs of pants, a few skirts, a dress or two?" Jessica suggested.

"Sure," Lila agreed, her face expressionless.

Jessica took Lila's arm and led her into Lisette's, an exclusive shop that specialized in imported goods.

Jessica stood in the middle of the store, taking in the new fashions. There was a whole wall of jeans in different colors and bins of T-shirts in pretty pastels. Chic pantsuits hung on circular racks in the middle of the store, and formal wear was displayed in the back. She chewed on a nail, wondering what part of Lila's wardrobe to attack first. "Do you want to go look at the dresses in back?" she asked.

"Why don't we just get some jeans first?" Lila suggested.

"Um, OK," Jessica agreed, feeling confused. Lila almost never wore jeans. In fact, it was her motto never to be seen in public in any kind of denim. "Blue jeans are for the masses," she was fond of saying. Jessica bit her lip as she followed Lila across the floor. Clearly she had lost her senses.

When they reached the jeans section, Jessica

ran a finger down the shelves, examining the selection. She stopped at a shelf of fashionable designer jeans. "Here, this is your size, right?" Jessica asked, looking at the label on a pair of white jeans.

Lila shifted her weight. "Yep, that's it."

Jessica held up the pants and studied them. "Do you want to try them on?" she asked.

Lila shook her head. "Nah, let's just take them." She reached up on the shelf and pulled out five pairs in different colors.

"Well, that was easy," Jessica muttered as they wandered down the aisle. She stopped at a circular rack of hanging shirts and dresses.

"Look, Li," Jessica said, fingering a row of elegant scoop-necked shirts that came in a variety of colors. "These are silk T-shirts. And they're made by Nadine. What do you think?" She pulled out a pale orange T-shirt and studied it.

"Sure, let's take them," Lila agreed.

Jessica stared at her friend in shock. Lila was the most particular shopper she knew. Not only did she wear the best designer clothes, but she had an impeccable sense of style. Now she couldn't care less. Jessica shook her head, wondering if this was a good idea. She was worried that Lila wouldn't want any of the stuff once she came out of her present funk.

Jessica replaced the T-shirt on the rack. "Lila, you don't really seem to be into this. Would you rather go shopping another day?" she asked.

"No, we might as well get this over with," Lila said. She turned to the medium section and picked out a few T-shirts, choosing one in each color.

"Besides, it's good to get away from Fowler Crest," Lila added, draping the shirts over her arm. "It's crawling with construction workers. And it's only going to get worse. I spent the whole day meeting with the lawyer for the estate. They're going to start the major reconstruction of the rooms tomorrow."

Jessica leafed through the rack, picking out a wine-colored silk shirt in Lila's size. "So they're going ahead with the renovations even though your parents are away?" she asked.

Lila nodded. "They're going to try to restore the mansion to its original form. But we're not going to do any redecorating until my parents get back. I can't make those decisions for them." Lila heaved a sigh. "I wish they were home already."

Jessica gave her a sympathetic smile. "Don't worry. They'll be back soon," she said.

"Yeah, I know," Lila said softly. But the sadness in her voice was evident.

Jessica bit her lip worriedly. She didn't know when she'd seen Lila so disheartened. She looked around the store quickly, hoping to find something that would really cheer her up. Finally she came upon a chic black linen pantsuit with a fitted waist and flared legs. It was perfect for Lila. "Hey, Li, what do you think of this?" she asked, holding it up.

Lila shook her head. "Nah, it's not really me." She glanced around the store. "I don't really see anything else I like. Why don't we just take what we've got and get out of here?"

"OK," Jessica agreed, following her to the counter. Lila laid her purchases next to the register and whipped out her credit card, throwing it down on the counter. "Good thing this didn't burn up, isn't it?" she asked dryly.

The saleswoman gave her a bright smile as she picked up the card. "Well, you've had a successful shopping day, now haven't you?" she asked.

Lila nodded, forcing a small smile.

After the saleswoman had wrapped up Lila's purchases in tissue paper, she filled up two big shopping bags. Jessica grabbed the heavier bag, which held the jeans, and Lila took the T-shirts.

"So do you want to go home now?" Lila asked as they walked out of the store.

"What?" Jessica exclaimed. "But we didn't get anything."

"Sure, we did," Lila said. "I've got enough jeans and T-shirts to last an entire month."

"But Lila, you have to get some nice clothes," Jessica protested. "Your entire wardrobe burned up."

Lila shrugged. "Well, it doesn't really matter all that much," she said.

Jessica's eyes almost popped out of her head. "I'm sorry— what did you say?"

Lila gazed into space. "You know, maybe Steven

114

was right," she said pensively. "Maybe I should be grateful for how much I *do* have."

Jessica wondered if she had heard right. Steven thought Lila should be grateful for her french-fried wardrobe? And Lila agreed? Something was very wrong.

Jessica grabbed hold of Lila's arm and steered her down the hall. She knew exactly what would get her best friend's mind off her troubles—Bibi's. It was an exclusive boutique that was way out of Jessica's price range.

"OK, one more stop and then we can go," Jessica said, leading Lila determinedly down the hall. She was sure Lila's spirits would pick up in the chic boutique. It was Lila's favorite store, and they had just put out a new collection.

Jessica stopped at the storefront window and gasped. An elegant array of pastel-colored dresses and suits was displayed. "Wow, look at the great colors!" Jessica exclaimed.

"Mmm, nice," Lila murmured.

"Oh, boy," Jessica muttered under her breath. This was going to be more difficult than she had realized.

But Jessica marched through the door. She headed down the aisle, fingering the fabrics. At the back of the store she spotted an absolutely beautiful floor-length evening gown. It was a shimmering emerald green, with delicate spaghetti straps and a fitted bodice. Of course, it was totally impractical, which made it ideal for Lila.

Jessica held it up to herself and whirled around. "Lila, you've got to try this on," she breathed. "It's stunning."

Lila shook her head. "Nah, I think we've got enough."

Jessica stared at her friend in consternation. "But all we got are jeans and T-shirts."

Lila shrugged. "Well, there's no room in the ruins of Fowler Crest to store any new stuff anyway."

"I'll keep the loot until you have room for it," Jessica offered.

Lila held up her hands. "OK, OK, I give up," she said. "But I really don't feel like trying on clothes." She sat down in a chair by the dressing room. "Why don't you try on the dress for both of us?"

Jessica slung the hanger over her arm. "Well, if you insist," she said with a sigh.

Jessica frowned as she headed for the dressing room. She didn't exactly mind trying on elegant evening wear, but they were supposed to be looking for clothes for Lila, not Jessica. At the moment, though, her best friend had absolutely no interest in shopping whatsoever. Lila was clearly in a serious depression.

Chapter 8

"OK, kids, it's time for bed!" Aunt Peggy announced, standing up and clapping. It was Tuesday evening, and the whole family was gathered in the living room, where Devon had been sleeping at night. The room was small and cozy, with an old brown foldout couch and a shaggy burnt orange rug.

Devon looked up from his newspaper, surprised at how quickly the evening had gone by. He was stretched out on the armchair, a glass of soda by his side. But apparently he was the only one who had heard his aunt's remark. Ross and Allan were lying on the rug in front of the television, engrossed in a sitcom. Uncle Mark was sitting at the table in the corner, an array of contracts spread out in front of him.

"Kids! I said it's bedtime!" Aunt Peggy repeated, her hands on her hips.

"Shhh! The program's almost over," Ross complained, his eyes glued to the TV.

Allan reached over and grabbed for the half-eaten bag of potato chips lying on the floor. Sitting up cross-legged, he stuffed a handful of chips in his mouth.

Aunt Peggy shook her head disapprovingly. "In my day kids used to *read* for entertainment," she said. "They didn't spend hours staring at a box."

"In your day people drove horses and buggies," Ross retorted.

Aunt Peggy pursed her lips, hiding a tiny smile. "Mark, did you hear what your son said?"

Uncle Mark looked up from the table. "Huh?" he asked.

"Nothing," Aunt Peggy said with a wave of her hand.

Devon laid the paper on his lap, smiling at the daily family bickering. He felt like he had entered Normaltown, U.S.A., and he was thrilled. Devon had spent the day with Uncle Mark, who had shown him the basics of his contracting business. After dinner he had played catch with Allan for an hour and then he had helped Ross with his biology homework. Devon was really beginning to feel like one of the family.

A commercial came on, and Aunt Peggy leaned over and clicked off the TV. "OK, show's over!" she said.

"Nice pun," Devon said with a grin.

Aunt Peggy gave him a grateful smile. "Well, at least *somebody* appreciates me around here."

Allan clicked the TV back on with the remote control.

Ross pulled himself up to a sitting position. "Aww, Mom, can't we just watch one more show?" he pleaded. Leaning over, he grabbed the remote control out of Allan's hand. Pointing it at the TV, he surfed quickly through the channels.

"Hey, stop there!" Allan cried out as Ross passed by the sports channel.

"No, I want to watch a talk show," Ross declared.

Allan grabbed the remote out of his brother's hand and jumped on the couch, holding it up in the air. "Sports or you're not getting this back," he warned.

Ross leapt up on the sofa and grabbed for the remote. Allan held it fast in his hand, waving it in the air. Ross lunged at him, and the two of them fell onto the couch. Soon a full-fledged fight ensued as the boys grappled wildly for the remote.

"Hey, what's going on here?" Uncle Mark growled, looking up from his work.

The kids stopped fighting and looked at their father. "Ross stole the clicker!" Allan complained, sliding off the couch.

"Allan's being an idiot!" Ross asserted.

"The kids are just going to bed," Aunt Peggy put in. She held out her hand palm up for the remote. Scowling, Allan handed it to her.

The kids reluctantly left the room. "Good night, Devon," Allan said on his way out, pouting slightly.

"Good night, Allan," Devon returned.

"Hey, race you upstairs," Ross said from the hallway.

The two of them charged up the steps.

Aunt Peggy shook her head. "Sometimes those kids can be a real handful."

"Well, they're at a pretty rowdy age," Devon said, folding up his newspaper and setting it aside.

"That's an understatement," Aunt Peggy said, taking a seat on the sofa. "Well, now that the boys are in bed, we can get down to serious business." The throw pillows were in disarray, and she rearranged them, plumping each one before she set it on the couch.

"Yes, Devon, we wanted to discuss your plans for the year," Uncle Mark said, coming over to join his wife on his couch. He sat back in the corner, flinging a strong arm over the side of the sofa.

Devon raised an eyebrow. "Oh?" he asked.

Aunt Peggy nodded. "I know you're still just adjusting to your new life here," she said. "But you should start thinking about going back to school." She reached up and patted her hair, which was swept up on top of her head as usual.

Devon nodded. "I've been thinking the same thing," he said.

"I spoke to the principal of Ross's school today,

and he said you could finish out your junior year here," Uncle Mark said.

"Hey, that's great!" Devon exclaimed, feeling strangely moved by the gesture. He wasn't used to people taking an interest in his life—or taking care of his life for him. He'd always been responsible for enrolling himself in school in Connecticut. "When can I start?"

"Well, no time like the present," Uncle Mark said, sitting forward on the edge of the couch. "Why don't we take a ride over to Clearwater High tomorrow and get you enrolled?"

Devon nodded. "OK," he agreed slowly. He hadn't expected everything to happen so fast. This was a very big step. Enrolling in school was a serious commitment. It meant he would really be staying in Ohio. And that he would be living with the Wilsons. It meant that he would have some stability at last.

"And you know, Devon," Aunt Peggy added casually, "since you're one of the family now, you should really have your own room."

Devon looked down, feeling a sudden rush of emotion. Tears came to his eyes, and he blinked them back. Feeling embarrassed by his unexpected reaction, he reached for his glass and took a big gulp of soda.

"We thought we'd add a wing to the downstairs, with a bathroom and everything," his aunt explained. "And since you've come into half of your inheritance, you won't even notice the cost," she added.

Devon almost choked on his soda.

"You don't mind, do you?" Uncle Mark asked.

"The house will be so much nicer," his aunt put in before he could respond. "I'll be so happy. And you will be too."

"More soda?" his uncle asked, holding up the bottle.

"Uh, sure," Devon muttered. He avoided his uncle's gaze as he refilled his glass.

"Well, we'd better let you turn in now," Uncle Mark said, standing abruptly and pulling Aunt Peggy along with him.

"Good night, dear," Aunt Peggy said. "Sleep well." She gave him a warm smile and shut the door softly behind them.

Devon stared at the door for a moment after they left, feeling as if he'd just been hit. Maybe his suspicions were on the mark after all, he thought. Maybe the Wilsons *did* just care about him for his money. Devon yanked open the foldout couch, feeling betrayed. Grabbing the blanket from the chair, he shook it out violently.

Devon switched off the lamp on the end table and crawled into bed. Lying flat on his back, he stared at the ceiling, trying to calm himself down.

It's not a big deal, Devon told himself. *It's just money.* And he had plenty of it to spare. He wouldn't even notice the cost of a few renovations.

Besides, he reassured himself, his aunt and uncle only had his best interests in mind. They really wanted him to be one of the family—with his own bedroom and his own bathroom. If they had the money, they would pay for his room themselves. Wouldn't they?

Steven lay on his bed Tuesday evening, pondering the latest development in the case. He had been turning it over in his mind all day. He just couldn't get over the fact that an empty gas can had been found in Lila's car. It was certainly an incriminating piece of evidence.

Steven turned on his side, propping his head up with his hand. Was it possible that Lila had actually set the fire herself? Narrowing his eyes, Steven tried to re-create the scene of the crime. He pictured Lila talking to the guy at the gas station, smiling sweetly as she purchased a can of gas. Then he saw her spraying gasoline liberally across the floors of the mansion, her hair loose and a wild expression on her face. Finally he imagined her sitting quietly in the living room, waiting calmly as the fire slowly burned away her home.

Steven sat up with a sigh. He just couldn't believe it. Lila seemed so innocent and stable. He couldn't imagine her committing such a crazy act.

And what would be in it for her? Steven asked himself. *What would she get out of it? Attention?* Steven shrugged. He had to admit that was a real possibility. It must be tough for a girl to be on her own like she was.

But one thing about the scenario was bothering him. If Lila had deliberately set her home on fire, then why hadn't she fled the scene of the crime? Why had she ended up alone in the living room, passed out from smoke inhalation?

Steven drummed his fingers on the bedspread, his mind racing. *Suicide?* he wondered. *Was the entire fire a suicide attempt?* Had Lila been trying to take her own life—and take her home down with her?

Steven stood up and crossed the room. He just couldn't figure it out. Was Lila a crafty arsonist, a lonely girl crying out for attention, an unstable teenager with suicidal tendencies? Or was she just the innocent victim of a cruel setup? Steven shook his head. One thing was certain—Lila Fowler was an enigma.

As Steven paced across the carpet his boss's words came back to him. *Lila Fowler may seem innocent, but you have to look deeper,* he heard his boss saying. *Don't let yourself be taken in by a pretty face.*

Steven paused, deep in thought. He had to take the D.A.'s advice seriously. After all, Joe Garrison was the best. He knew what he was talking about. Maybe Lila *was* just using her feminine wiles to put him off track. Maybe this was all just a ploy to get the heat off her.

124

And if that was the case, Steven realized, it was working. He sank down on the side of the bed, staring into space. Lila Fowler was definitely playing on his heartstrings. He woke up thinking about her, and he went to bed thinking about her. And he had to admit that his interest in her was *not* entirely business.

Steven frowned. Was it possible? Was he really interested in one of his sister's friends? He shook his head. If someone had told him a few weeks ago that he would get emotionally involved with rich, spoiled Lila Fowler, he would have told them they were stark raving mad.

He bit his lip, imagining how Jessica would react if she knew what he was thinking. She would be totally disgusted with him. *And who could blame her?* Steven thought. After all, Lila was his sister's best friend. She was completely off territory.

Steven made a firm resolve to harden himself to her. From this moment on, he and Lila would have a strictly lawyer-client relationship. He wouldn't let her get to him. He would only be interested in facts, facts, facts.

For the moment the most important item to look into was the empty gas can. Steven decided to call Lila to investigate the latest twist. He reached for the phone, determined to be businesslike. He wasn't sure if the phone lines had been reconnected, but Lila had bought a cellular phone for the pool house. Flicking on his phone, he flipped through his notebook for Lila's number.

Despite his resolve he didn't feel professional at all as he punched in the numbers. His heart was hammering in his chest as if he were about to ask her out on a date.

Steven Wakefield, get ahold of yourself, he told himself as the phone rang.

"Hello?" Lila answered. She sounded out of breath.

Steven cleared his throat and put on a professional voice. "Hello, Lila, this is Steven Wakefield."

"Steven!" Lila responded happily.

Steven felt his pulse pick up and drew a long breath.

Just then Elizabeth knocked lightly on the door and poked her head through the doorway.

"Uh, Lila, can you hold on a minute?" Steven asked, covering the receiver with his hand.

"Oh, sorry," Elizabeth said as she saw he was on the phone. "I just wanted to know if you wanted to watch a movie with me and Todd tomorrow night."

Steven blinked, feeling strangely guilty. "Oh, sure," he said.

"Great!" Elizabeth said, giving him a big smile and shutting the door.

"The women in your life bothering you?" Lila asked flirtatiously.

Steven could feel his face turning red. "Uh, yeah," he said, coughing. Then he cleared his throat again and tried to regain his composure. "Lila, there have been some important developments in the case that I need to discuss with you."

"Have they found the arsonist?" Lila asked hopefully.

"Unfortunately not," Steven responded. He stood up, gripping the phone tightly.

"Did something happen? Am I in danger?" Lila asked. The anxiety in her voice was clear, and Steven felt his heart go out to her.

"No, no, nothing like that," Steven reassured her, taking a seat in his desk chair. "But I can't talk about it over the phone. Can I come by tomorrow night to meet with you?"

Lila sighed. "I don't think so," she said. "This place has been transformed into a construction site, and they're working day and night. There's way too much hammering and drilling for us to have a meeting here."

Steven paused in thought. "Well, I would suggest my office, but you've got school tomorrow."

"How about dinner?" Lila proposed casually.

Steven hesitated. He didn't know if dinner was a good idea. He wanted to meet in a professional environment, not an intimate restaurant. But then, he really didn't have much of a choice. "Sure," he agreed finally.

"Why don't I pick you up after work tomorrow?" Lila offered.

"Uh, OK," Steven said slowly. "How about six o'clock?"

"Great, it's a date," Lila said lightly.

A *date?* Steven wondered as he hung up the phone. *Is it?* No, of course not. It was a business meeting. He was just doing his job. Attorneys took their clients out to dinner all the time.

But despite his attempt to reassure himself, his feelings were telling him a different story. His face was flushed, and his heart was racing. Lila's voice echoed in his mind, evoking a strange mixture of danger and desire.

There was no denying it. He was falling for Lila Fowler.

Did she do it or didn't she? Steven wondered to himself. He couldn't quite decide. And he had to admit that the mystery only heightened his growing attraction to her.

Watch out, Wakefield, Steven told himself. *You may be playing with fire.*

Chapter 9

"That history test was totally impossible!" Jessica complained, leaning against an aluminum locker on Wednesday afternoon at Sweet Valley High.

"It was completely unfair," Amy agreed, shaking her head. "I can't believe Mr. Jaworski expected us to know all the dates of the battles in the Civil War."

Lila turned the dial on her combination lock, feeling completely removed from her friends' conversation. Her first day back at school was turning out to be even worse than she'd thought. Everybody was staring at her as if they expected to see burn marks covering her entire body, and students whispered to one another when she walked by.

"When do you have to make up the test?" Jessica asked Lila.

"Actually I don't have to make it up," Lila

responded, pulling open her locker door. "Mr. Jaworski said he would just let it go, seeing as how I was suffering from a difficult emotional trauma." Lila reached into her locker and grabbed her intermediate French book.

"You're so lucky!" Jessica exclaimed.

Lila tucked her books underneath her arm, giving Jessica a sharp look. "I wouldn't exactly say that," she said dryly. She slammed her locker door shut.

"In a certain manner of speaking, of course," Jessica said, amending her words quickly.

Just then Caroline Pearce passed and did a double take. "Lila!" she gushed, rushing up to them. "How *are* you?" she asked. She laid a sympathetic hand on Lila's arm and gave her a big smile.

Lila gritted her teeth, fighting off the urge to swat Caroline's claws off her arm. A tall girl with red hair and ivory skin, Caroline had a notorious reputation as the class gossip. Lila was sure her interest wasn't purely altruistic.

"I'm fine," Lila said, giving Caroline a sugary smile.

Caroline studied Lila's face, clearly looking for signs of damage. "Well, you look great," she said. "You were really lucky to get through the accident without any burns, huh?"

"Yep," Lila said, shrugging Caroline's hand away nonchalantly. "I sure was."

Caroline brought her head next to Lila's. She

was so close that Lila could feel the heat emanating from her body. She was wearing a sickly sweet perfume with a heady scent. Feeling as if she were suffocating, Lila quickly took a step back. "Have they had any luck in finding the arsonist?" Caroline asked in a low voice.

Lila could feel her blood boiling. The fire was absolutely none of Caroline Pearce's business. Lila closed her eyes and quickly counted to ten in her mind. She knew if she responded defensively, Caroline would take that as a definite sign of trouble. Then even worse rumors would be all over school tomorrow.

"I'm not sure," Lila said, fighting to keep her equanimity. "I believe the investigation is highly confidential."

"But surely they would keep you informed," Caroline pressed her.

Lila grabbed onto her locker for support. This girl was really too much.

"Listen, we've really got to be going now," Jessica cut in. "We'll be late for class." Lila gave her a grateful smile.

"See you, Caroline," Lila said, heading down the hall with her friends.

"See you!" Caroline waved. "And let's have lunch soon, OK?" she asked.

"Sure, I'd love to," Lila called back, a fake smile plastered on her face.

Lila rolled her eyes as soon as Caroline was out

of sight. "She's like the hundredth person who has approached me today to get information about the fire," she complained.

"Well, I guess that's normal," Amy put in, jumping to adjust her leather backpack. "Everybody wants to make sure you're OK."

But Lila shook her head. "I don't think that's it," she countered. "Everybody's treating me like I'm some kind of freak."

They passed the water fountain, where some freshman girls were gathered. As Lila and her friends turned the corner the group suddenly got quiet. A few whispers could be heard, and a freshman girl even pointed right at Lila. "Is that her?" the girl asked in a loud whisper.

"You see!" Lila exclaimed triumphantly. "I feel like an animal in the zoo!"

"You *do* seem to be attracting a lot of attention," Jessica conceded.

"Listen, Lila, don't let it get to you," Amy counseled her. "You know how the gossip network is here. Everybody is so bored, they're just looking for something to talk about."

"Yeah, Amy's right," Jessica put in. "This is sure to be yesterday's news in no time."

Lila heaved a deep sigh. "Well, I hope so," she said. She stopped when they reached the end of the hall, shifting her books in her arms. The girls had to go in different directions for their next classes. Jessica and Amy had English together, and

Lila had French class. "I'll talk to you guys later, OK?" Lila added.

"I'll call you," Jessica said, holding her hand up to her ear as if she had a receiver in her hand.

"And don't let them get to you!" Amy added.

The girls waved and walked away.

Lila hurried down the hall, holding her books close to her chest. She couldn't wait for this day to be over. All she wanted to do was go home and hide, far away from the curious glances of the students at Sweet Valley High.

A shadow fell across her path, and Lila looked back quickly, her heart rate accelerating. But nobody was there. It was odd, but whenever she was alone, it seemed like she was being followed. Every time Lila turned a corner, she had the eerie feeling that there was a presence right behind her. It was like she had a permanent shadow. But when she looked, nobody was ever there.

Lila, you're just being paranoid, she berated herself. But still, she couldn't help glancing around nervously and picking up her pace.

Lila walked quickly past a group of sophomore boys who were waiting in front of a classroom. She could feel them looking her over curiously, and she could hear them whispering quietly among themselves. Lila straightened up and marched past them, holding her head high.

She turned the corner and was about to enter her French class but stopped short, sure she saw a fleeting shadow disappear. She looked back quickly but of course saw no one.

Lila leaned against the wall and put her hands to her head. Was she losing her mind? Was she becoming a nervous wreck?

Lila closed her eyes and took a deep breath. Just one more class, and then she was free. And she was going to see Steven after school. She was sure he'd make her feel better. She was sure he'd make the ghosts disappear.

"Where in the world *is* he?" Elizabeth complained. It was Wednesday evening, and she and Todd were settled together on the love seat in the den, waiting for Steven. They'd rented two Hitchcock movies at the video store, and they'd made a batch of popcorn. Now they just needed Steven to show up to get the evening started.

"Oh, you're wondering where Steven is?" Todd asked, an expression of mock innocence on his face.

Elizabeth couldn't help smiling. She'd been repeating the refrain like a mantra for the last hour. "But he *said* he'd join us," Elizabeth said, glancing at her watch. It was almost eight o'clock. Steven should have been home hours ago.

"I hate to break it to you, Liz, but I think we're being stood up," Todd said.

Elizabeth heaved a sigh. "I guess you're right," she admitted.

Just then Mrs. Wakefield popped her head in the den. She was wearing jeans and a yellow cable-knit sweater, and a light blue scarf was tied around her head, bringing out the color in her sparkling blue eyes. With her youthful outfit she looked like she could have been the twins' older sister rather than their mother. "Hi, kids, do you need anything?" she asked.

Elizabeth sighed, crossing her legs at the knee. "Just Steven."

Mrs. Wakefield's forehead crinkled in confusion. "Huh?"

Elizabeth scowled. "Steven said he'd watch a movie with us tonight."

Mrs. Wakefield crossed the den and picked up an empty pitcher from the side table. "Well, dear, I'm sure he'll be along any minute now," she said, heading to the door. "If you need anything, Dad and I are just upstairs."

"Thanks, Mom," Elizabeth said.

"Good night, Mrs. Wakefield," Todd added.

"Good night, kids," Mrs. Wakefield responded, giving them a gentle smile. Then she shut the door softly behind her.

"So, should I put in a movie?" Todd asked, picking up the tapes. "We've got *Vertigo* and *Rear Window*—both sizzling romantic thrillers." He gave her a comical wink. "Which would you prefer?"

But Elizabeth had barely heard him. She stood

135

up and paced the shaggy carpet in the den, deep in thought. "Do you think Steven could still be at work?" she asked. "Maybe he got caught up in the Fowler Crest case and hasn't noticed the time."

Todd sighed and fell back on the couch.

Elizabeth ran her fingers through her golden blond hair, nodding to herself. "I'm sure that's it," she said. "That's exactly what happens to my dad when he's working really hard on a case, and Steven is just like him."

Elizabeth plopped down in the armchair in the corner and reached for the phone. She sat back and placed the console in her lap, punching in a few numbers.

Todd looked at her in alarm. "Liz! What are you doing?"

"Shhh!" she said, holding up an index finger. "Yes, I'd like the number of the Sweet Valley District Attorney's office. . . . OK, thank you."

Holding the receiver in the crook of her neck, Elizabeth grabbed a small pad from the table next to her and scrawled down the number. Then she hung up and picked up the receiver again.

"Liz! Wait!" Todd said, jumping up. "You can't call Steven at work."

"And why not?" Elizabeth asked, looking at him quizzically as she replaced the receiver in the cradle.

"Because . . . because he has the right to his privacy," Todd stuttered. "Steven's a grown man.

You're not his mother or his girlfriend."

Elizabeth's mouth dropped open. "So is that what girlfriends do? They follow their boyfriends around like mother hens?"

Todd grinned. "Yes, exactly," he said. He crinkled his forehead in distress. "We need our freedom!" he added, flinging his arms out dramatically.

Elizabeth shook her head at her boyfriend's antics. "Well, now I really am going to call," she said, picking up the receiver.

But Todd leapt on top of her and grabbed for the phone.

"To-odd!" Elizabeth exclaimed, holding the receiver out of his reach.

Todd quickly plucked the phone number out of her other hand, crumpling it up and throwing it to the floor. "Do you surrender?" he asked.

"Never!" Elizabeth said, wildly fighting him off.

Todd sat on top of her and gently pinned her arms down by her sides. "Now?" he asked.

Elizabeth couldn't help giggling. "Todd, stop it!" she said, trying to sound mad. "My parents are upstairs. They're going to think we're having a fight."

Todd smiled. "Well, then, you'd better stop making a scene."

Elizabeth shook her head, but she quieted down.

As soon as she stopped struggling Todd leaned in and began kissing her neck. Elizabeth let the receiver drop from her hand and closed her eyes, enjoying the warm feel of Todd's lips as they traced a trail along her neck.

When Todd pulled back, his coffee brown eyes were burning with a liquid fire. "See, it's kind of nice to have a night alone together, isn't it?"

"Mmm," Elizabeth agreed, leaning forward and kissing him softly.

Todd kissed her back, smiling at her tenderly. "So can we watch that romantic thriller now?"

"OK," Elizabeth agreed. "Why don't you get the popcorn from the kitchen while I set up the VCR?"

"Anything for you, princess," Todd agreed, kissing her gently on the cheek. Then he unfolded his muscular legs from the armchair and headed down the hall to the kitchen.

As soon as Todd was out of sight, Elizabeth grabbed the crumpled-up piece of paper from the floor and smoothed it out on her lap. Slouching down in her seat so Todd couldn't see her, she quickly placed a call to the D.A.'s office. But the phone just rang and rang. Then a recording came on saying that the office was closed. Elizabeth set the phone down in disappointment.

"Tsk, tsk, tsk," Todd said, shaking his head in disapproval as he walked back into the room, a huge wooden bowl of popcorn in his hand.

"What is this? Are you my mother? Or my girlfriend?" Elizabeth retorted with a grin.

"I'm just trying to protect you—from yourself," Todd said, setting the popcorn on the low coffee table in front of the couch.

"Well, he wasn't there anyway," Elizabeth said.

"So does that mean you're giving up the search?" Todd asked, grabbing a handful of popcorn from the bowl and stuffing it in his mouth.

"I guess so," Elizabeth said slowly. She picked up the videos and glanced at the backs. *Vertigo* OK with you?" she asked, heading to the TV. Todd nodded and dimmed the lights. Kneeling down, she inserted the tape in the VCR. Then she rejoined Todd on the couch.

Elizabeth sighed. "It's just that I'm really worried about him," she said. "I hope he's not sitting alone in some diner, moping about Billie." She took a handful of popcorn and dropped a few pieces in her mouth.

"Well, maybe he needs some time to himself to think things over," Todd said, grabbing a fluffy blue blanket from the edge of the couch and throwing it over them.

"Yeah, maybe you're right," Elizabeth said as she snuggled closer to Todd. "And maybe some time alone will make him realize he should get back together with Billie."

Todd put his arm around her shoulders. "Liz, really, I'm sure he's fine," he reassured her. "He probably just wants to be alone."

Todd leaned over and kissed her softly on the

cheek. Elizabeth closed her eyes, feeling herself relax as Todd covered her cheek in featherlight kisses. Then she turned and captured his lips in hers. Soon all thoughts of Steven were far from her mind.

"Lila, don't you think this is a bit upscale for a business meeting?" Steven commented nervously as Lila turned into the parking lot at Chez Costa on Wednesday evening. Chez Costa was a fancy French restaurant in downtown Sweet Valley.

"I insist," Lila said lightly, pulling her lime green Triumph adeptly into a spot. "Dinner's on me."

"No, Lila, I can't let you do that," Steven protested.

But Lila turned to look at him with imploring eyes. "Steven, I really want to do something for you to thank you for all your support," she said. "I don't know how I would have gotten through this without you."

Steven sighed. "OK," he reluctantly agreed.

As they walked across the parking lot, Steven wondered again if this was a good idea. He was flattered that Lila wanted to take him out, but he was afraid that she had misunderstood his intentions.

This evening was turning out to look a lot like a date, Steven thought worriedly. Lila was taking him to dinner at one of the most romantic, intimate restaurants in town, and she looked lovely. She had on an elegant midnight blue evening dress that she had borrowed from Jessica, and her hair was swept up on her head in a graceful twist. She wasn't wearing any jewelry, which only added to the classic simplicity of the look.

"It feels good to get out," Lila had said brightly when she picked him up. "I even dressed up for the occasion." But Steven wasn't sure that was her only motivation. Had she dressed up for the restaurant or had she dressed up for *him?*

Steven held open the door for Lila and followed her inside. His eyes widened as he took in the fancy decor. The restaurant was done in shades of rose, with pale pink walls and a deep red carpet. A crystal chandelier hung above their heads, and impressionist art adorned the walls. The only sounds that could be heard were the low hush of voices and the quiet tinkling of wineglasses.

Steven bit his lip, feeling completely out of his element. He was used to campus burger joints or casual diners. And most of the time he and Billie just cooked spaghetti at home.

The maitre d' stood behind a rich oak stand, a large reservation book open in front of him. He bowed slightly as they approached him. "Good evening," he said.

"Dinner for two," Lila said quietly. "We have a reservation under Fowler."

The maitre d' smiled respectfully. "Right this way, please."

They followed him across the dimly lit room to a romantic, square table in the corner. An elegant white tablecloth was draped over the top, and two round pink candles were set out in small glass jars. A tiny rose stood in a crystal vase in the middle of the table.

"Your waiter will be with you in a moment," the maitre d' said, placing two menus on the table. With a click of his heels he turned and walked away.

Lila reached for the matches in the ashtray and struck a match, leaning forward to light the candles. She looked mesmerized as she set the wicks on fire. The candles cast a rosy tint on her pale skin, and her brown eyes danced in the light. Steven blinked. Was he imagining things, or was she taking an extreme pleasure in lighting the candles?

"I love the glow of candlelight," Lila affirmed, gazing at the tiny flames with a dreamy smile.

Steven bit his lip, wondering if this was significant.

"So why don't we get whatever business you wanted to discuss over with right away?" Lila said, turning to him with a bright smile. "Then we can enjoy our meal." She sat back and crossed her legs. "That's what my father always says—business first, pleasure later."

Steven felt his face flush. Was this business or

pleasure? That was the question. And he had to admit to himself that he hoped it was both.

Steven shook his head, trying to remember his resolve to be businesslike. He cleared his throat and put a serious expression on his face. "Apparently a new piece of evidence was found by some detectives on the case—an empty gas can."

Lila nodded, her eyes narrowed in thought. "Well, I guess that's not surprising," she surmised. "I mean, after all, somebody did pour gasoline all over the house."

"The gas can was found in your car," Steven said softly.

Lila shrugged, unconcerned. "Oh, well, then it probably doesn't have anything to do with the case. The chauffeur must have left a can of spare gas in my Triumph. He drives my car too."

Steven nodded, studying Lila's face, but her expression didn't change. And nothing in her behavior betrayed her calm. *She seems so nonchalant*, Steven thought. *Can she really be such a good actress?*

Steven sat back in his chair. "Well, I'll have to talk to the chauffeur," he stated.

"Yes, sir, Mr. D.A., sir," Lila said flirtatiously.

Steven felt himself blushing again and grabbed for his water glass. He took a big gulp, trying to cool down. Lila Fowler had an incredible power over him. As soon as she turned on her charm he melted.

But then Lila's expression turned serious. "Steven, you can talk to anyone in the household," she said. "I want you to do whatever it takes to catch the arsonist." A flicker of worry appeared in her light brown eyes. She frowned and looked away.

"Hey, what's wrong?" Steven asked, leaning forward. "Did something happen in school today?"

Lila heaved a sigh. "Well, I don't know," she said, her brow crinkling. "Maybe I'm being paranoid, but I had the distinct feeling that somebody was following me all day."

Steven felt a pang of fear in his chest. Despite his boss's suspicions, Steven believed that his *own* theory was right. He thought somebody was after Lila. Steven reached out and covered her hand with his. "Lila, I doubt you're being paranoid," he said, looking deep into her eyes. "But don't worry—I'm with you. I won't let anything happen to you."

Lila smiled gratefully, a few tears sparkling like diamonds in her eyes.

Lila's face glowed in the candlelight, and her delicate hand felt warm under his. Steven longed to take her in his arms, to wipe away her pain and fear, to kiss away her tears. . . .

"So have you decided yet?" a male voice asked.

Steven blinked and looked up, pulling his hand away from Lila's. A young waiter in a black tuxedo was standing over them, smiling politely.

"Uh, well, do you know what you want?" Steven asked Lila.

"Why don't we start with a dozen oysters?" Lila suggested, her eyes twinkling with good humor again.

"Very good," the waiter said with a nod, scratching down the order on his pad.

"And what's the plat du jour?" Lila asked, speaking with a perfect French accent.

"Today's specialty is roast duck with asparagus in a mustard vinaigrette sauce," the waiter said. "I highly recommend it."

Lila looked over at Steven. "How does that sound to you?"

"Perfect," Steven said, watching Lila in admiration. She was completely at ease in the elegant setting. It was obvious that she had been ordering in fancy restaurants all her life.

"You know, I once dug for oysters in the south of France," Lila remarked when the waiter had left. "You wouldn't believe how slippery they are," she said with a giggle. "I almost fell in the water trying to retrieve one."

Steven couldn't help smiling back. When Lila was happy, her whole face lit up.

"That was quite a trip," Lila said, her face animated with the recollection. "First my parents and I stayed in this tiny fishing village in the south of France, sailing all morning in the Mediterranean and fishing in the afternoon. And then we went to

Monaco and were swept away in a series of balls with the royalty." Lila waved an elegant hand in the air. "To tell you the truth, I liked the French fishermen better. They really live life, and they had great stories to tell. Princes and princesses can get really tiresome."

Steven swallowed hard. Lila was talking about her vacation with royalty as casually as he would talk about a camping trip. She was only sixteen, and she had already seen more of the world than he had.

The waiter arrived with a platter of gray oysters, which he set down in the middle of the table. Then he placed two china plates in front of them. Picking up the serving spoon, he dished out a spoonful of oysters and filled both of their plates. *"Bon appétit,"* he said as he left.

Steven eyed the platter with apprehension. He had never eaten oysters in a restaurant before, and he wasn't really sure how to get them out of their shells without making a huge mess. He decided to watch Lila and take his cues from her.

Lila picked up her plastic bib and tucked it in her dress. "This is the most important part," she said with a grin. "Oysters may be a luxury, but they sure are *messy.*"

Steven tucked in his bib as well, feeling more and more impressed with Lila. Not only was she worldly and cultivated, but she was down-to-earth as well. She was nothing like he'd thought she was.

He had thought she was just a superficial snob, but obviously he'd been way off the mark.

Lila stuck her miniature fork in one of the shells, wedging out the meat. "So what's college like?" she asked. "It must be nice to be on your own."

Steven cocked his head. "But you're already sort of on your own, aren't you?" he asked. He picked up his fork too, frowning as he struggled to get an oyster out of its shell.

Lila shook her head. "It's not the same thing. I'm still in high school, and I still live at home. At college you really have your independence." She brought her fork to her mouth and took a delicate bite.

Steven nodded, managing to get out the meat without shooting it across the table. "That's true." He bit into the salty oyster, thinking about her question. "College is great. There are lots of parties, and there are always interesting political demonstrations going on, but it's also a lot of work."

"You're studying law?" Lila inquired. She picked up her napkin and dabbed at the corners of her mouth.

Steven nodded. "Well, I'm prelaw for the moment." He reached for a wedge of lemon from the serving dish and squirted it over his plate.

"What kind of law are you interested in?" Lila asked, picking up her water glass and taking a sip.

"I think I'd like to go into public interest law," Steven said. "You know, work for the community or the underprivileged or something."

Lila nodded, a small smile on her lips. "I'm not surprised," she said. "I had you pegged as the white knight type."

Lila gazed up at him, and their eyes met. Steven felt his whole body get hot. Lila's lips were red and soft in the glow of the candlelight, and they were parted slightly in a small smile. Steven moved forward instinctively. Then he jerked himself back.

What are you thinking? he berated himself. *This is business. Business, business, business,* he repeated in his mind.

The waiter arrived with two steaming platters of roast duck. He set down their dishes in front of them and picked up the oyster tray. "Enjoy your meal," he said.

"This looks delicious," Steven remarked, eyeing the gourmet dish appreciatively. But he couldn't help feeling a twinge of apprehension at the same time. The last time he'd had a fancy meal was months ago, when he'd taken Billie out to an Italian restaurant for her birthday. But it hadn't been nearly as nice as this. And Lila was paying for the whole thing on top of it.

"Bon appétit!" Lila said with a grin, cutting into her entrée.

Two hours later they had finished their meal.

They'd followed up dinner with chocolate mousse cake and espresso. Steven didn't know when he'd enjoyed himself more. The gourmet meal had actually been relatively painless. The food was extraordinary, and Lila's company was enchanting. The evening had flown by. Before he knew it, it was eleven o'clock.

"Steven, thank you," Lila said as they headed for the door. "You've really cheered me up."

"*I* should thank *you*," Steven said. "I haven't had such a nice evening in a long time."

But Lila shook her head. "No," she said softly. "I could never repay you for what you've done for me."

As they passed the front desk the maître d' bowed slightly. "*Bonsoir*," he said.

"*Bonsoir*," Lila responded, taking a box of matches from the bowl on the stand.

Steven's eyes widened, and he looked at her for an explanation. But she just tucked the matches in her purse and pushed open the door. Steven followed her out of the restaurant, feeling worried again.

The night was cool and balmy with a clear, deep blue sky, and there was a slight breeze in the air. Lila pulled her scarf tightly around her shoulders.

"What are the matches for?" Steven asked casually as they walked across the lot.

"Oh, it's just a little souvenir," Lila responded lightly. "I always take matches from restaurants."

Steven absorbed the information with alarm.

Lila loved candlelight, and she collected matches. He thought of her expression as she had lit the candles in the restaurant. She had looked almost hypnotized. *Is she a pyromaniac?* Steven wondered. *Is she playing with him? Is this some kind of cat-and-mouse game?*

"After all, I've got to start rebuilding my memories," Lila said. "And no time like the present to start, right?"

Lila turned and gave him a bright smile, a smile that was just for him. Steven's pulse picked up at her affectionate gaze. And the note of danger just made his heart beat faster.

Chapter 10

Devon stood outside on Thursday afternoon, watching the work being done on the house. His aunt and uncle hadn't wasted any time. An entire new wing was already in the works. Construction workers with hard hats were drilling holes in the ground, and men in overalls were constructing a frame out of long wooden planks.

A pile of plastic milk crates were cluttered under the tree where Devon was standing. He grabbed one and sat down on it, feeling a bit uneasy.

Everything was moving so fast, he thought. Yesterday he and Uncle Mark had driven over to Clearwater High School. It was an ugly modern building with long corridors and rows of steel gray lockers. The place had no atmosphere, but the principal had greeted him warmly and had enrolled him in the junior class. Devon would

151

start school on Monday. And his new bedroom would be ready in a week.

On Monday my new life begins, Devon thought. He was going to be part of a normal family in a normal town. But for some reason he didn't feel so enthusiastic about it anymore. He was beginning to feel like he was in too deep. His instincts told him to get out now, while he still could.

Devon picked up a twig and drew a line in the dirt, wondering why he felt so suspicious. *You're too cynical,* he berated himself. *You have to learn to trust people.*

Just then Ross and Allan came running across the lawn. They had just gotten home from school and were carrying canvas backpacks over their shoulders. Devon could see a big yellow school bus pulling away from the curb.

"Hey, Devon, we need your help!" Ross said when they reached him. He was out of breath, and his light blue eyes were sparkling.

"Sure, what is it?" Devon asked, putting the twig in his mouth and chewing on the end of it.

Ross crouched down in front of him. "Well, everybody's been talking about you in school today," he said. "They all want to know who the new cool guy is." Ross's light brown hair fell over his forehead, and he pushed it back with a dirty hand.

Devon groaned under his breath. He was hoping to be anonymous at his new school, just a regular guy from a regular family. He was sick of being a celebrity with rich parents and a genius IQ. "And what did you tell them?" he asked warily.

"I said you were my new big brother," Ross said, his eyes shining.

"And that's it?" Devon asked, narrowing his eyes suspiciously.

"Yeah," Ross said, looking confused.

Devon chewed on the edge of the twig, relieved. It didn't sound like Ross had given much away. "So what can I do for you?"

"We want to be more like you!" Allan exclaimed, dancing around him. He pulled his baseball mitt out of his backpack and jammed his hand into it.

Devon blinked in surprise. "How are you going to do that?" he asked, throwing the stick across the lawn.

Ross stood up and took a few steps across the lawn, rubbing his hands together. "Well, I've got a little plan to turn into Mr. Cool and Popular," he explained. "All I need is a new set of wheels and a new wardrobe. I'll look totally hot on a slick black motorbike." Ross grinned. "The girls won't be able to resist me."

Tiny alarms went off in Devon's head. He knew what that meant. In order to get a new motorbike and a bunch of new clothes, Ross needed money—Devon's money.

"And I'd need some dating advice from you as well," Ross added.

Well, at least the advice is free, Devon thought ironically.

Ross looked at him hopefully. "So what do you say?" he asked.

Devon was tempted to refuse, but then he softened. Ross was just a kid. Devon was sure his intentions were innocent. And a motorbike and some clothes wouldn't cost much. Devon wouldn't even notice it. "Sure," Devon said, standing up. "I'll be happy to help you out."

"You would?" Ross responded. He jumped up and down and let out a small whoop.

"That's not fair!" Allan cried, throwing his baseball from one hand to the other. "If you get all new stuff, then so should I!"

Devon sighed inwardly. "What do you need, Allan?"

Allan pulled his baseball hat low over his forehead. He moved closer to Devon and spoke in a low voice. "Well, you see, I have this new girlfriend who loves mountain biking," he began.

"You have a girlfriend?" Ross interrupted.

Allan's lips turned down in a pout. "Shut up!" he exclaimed. "It's none of your business!" Turning his back to his brother, he faced Devon with a sincere expression on his face. "If I don't get a bike soon, she's going to dump me for someone else."

"You got it," Devon said with a smile.

Allan's eyes widened. "Really? One of those state-of-the-art mountain bikes with climbing bars and off-road tires?"

Devon nodded. "Exactly. One of those."

"Oh, boy!" Allan breathed.

"Let's go tell Mom!" Ross put in.

"Thanks, Devon!" the boys exclaimed, running off excitedly.

Devon leaned back against a tree trunk and crossed his arms over his chest. He wasn't sure what to think. He wanted to hold on to the idea of his perfect relatives. He wanted to believe he was part of the family.

Devon squinted thoughtfully. If a few material items made them happy, it wasn't a big deal. After all, his cousins never had much money. He couldn't blame them for wanting a few things. And Devon could afford to be generous. He had ten million dollars to his name.

Just then a construction worker approached the area and reached for one of the milk crates. He was wearing a hard hat, and his face was smeared with dirt.

"How're you doing?" Devon asked, moving out of his way.

"I'm all right," the man responded lazily. "But I don't know about you." He had a slight southern twang to his voice.

Devon looked at him questioningly. "Huh?" he asked.

"I heard it's your money that's paying for all of this," the man said, standing with his arms folded across his chest and his legs far apart. "Pret-ty generous of you."

Devon shrugged, feeling uncomfortable. His personal affairs were none of this guy's business. And he didn't like people knowing about his wealth.

The man shifted his crate to the other hand and leaned in closer to Devon. "Looks like this family of yours is milking you for all you're worth."

Devon gave him a sharp look. "What are you talking about?" he responded defensively. "We're family. Families share what they've got."

The worker shrugged. "Where I come from, it's called *stealing*," he drawled. Then he turned and sauntered away.

Devon frowned after the worker had left. He stood up and headed into the house, the man's comment echoing in his mind. Was he sharing or were they stealing? Did his relatives really consider him one of the family? Or were they just using him to improve their lifestyle?

Jessica sat on the floor in her bedroom on Thursday night, painting her toenails. She and Lila had gone shopping again that afternoon, and she was surrounded by Lila's purchases. Shopping bags were lined up along the rug, and clothing was draped over every available surface.

Jessica's purple bedroom was normally a disaster zone. Her clothes tended to be piled up knee-deep on the floor, and fashion magazines and CDs were usually scattered all over the rug. Before their shopping spree had begun, Jessica's room had already been cluttered. Now she could barely get across the floor.

Jessica nudged aside a box and lifted her left foot in the air, bending down carefully to apply ruby red polish on her big toe. As she painted the rest of her toenails, she went over the purchases of the day. She had managed to talk Lila into buying a few nice pairs of pants and a handful of dresses. They'd even bought a chic, short black raincoat and a couple of pairs of shoes.

Jessica surveyed the crammed space, wondering how she would manage to fit any more stuff in her room. The place was literally full to bursting. And she'd promised Lila they'd go accessory shopping this weekend. It looked like she was going to have to start using Elizabeth's room as well.

Actually, Jessica thought with a sigh, she hadn't exactly promised Lila she would go shopping. Lila had promised *her* she'd go shopping. Jessica had practically had to beg her friend to accompany her. Despite all their purchases Jessica's consumer campaign wasn't going very successfully. Lila seemed to be somewhere else. She was basically letting Jessica shop for her and just trailing along.

Jessica bit her lip as she turned to her other foot. She was worried that Lila wouldn't want any of the clothes once she returned to her normal self. After all, they weren't really Lila's style. Jessica was the one who picked out the clothes, and Jessica was the one who tried them on. She had the disturbing feeling that *she* was going to be the one who ended up with a new wardrobe.

Of course, Jessica had to admit, she wouldn't be terribly upset if Lila gave her all the clothes. She had made some terrific purchases. They'd bought a gorgeous black wool pantsuit and a couple of beautiful long wraparound skirts.

But that wasn't the point, Jessica said to herself, waving her left foot in the air to dry her toes. The whole point of this excursion had been to cheer Lila up. And the project was clearly a failure.

On the other hand, Jessica thought, maybe her attempts hadn't completely bombed. Lila *was* beginning to take an interest in clothes again. She had stopped by on Wednesday after school and had borrowed Jessica's long blue dress. Jessica frowned, wondering why Lila had wanted an evening dress. But Lila had been completely mysterious about the whole thing. She had just smiled enigmatically and waltzed out of the house with the dress slung over her arm.

Jessica sighed and leaned back against the bed, worried about her best friend. Lila was completely unreachable at the moment. Usually she turned to Jessica when she was depressed or upset about something, but now she was in her own little world. She didn't want to talk about the fire, and she didn't want to talk about her feelings. She seemed to be a million miles away.

Removing the cotton balls from between her toes, Jessica pondered how she was going to get Lila to snap out of it. Clearly shopping wasn't the answer. Lila obviously wasn't her good old materialistic self at the moment.

Jessica stood up and stepped among the packages, her eyes narrowed in thought. There must be some way to make Lila feel better. There must be some way to replace what had been lost in the fire.

That's it, Jessica realized, sinking down on the side of the bed. She had to replace something that mattered to Lila. She had to bring back something of the past. Jessica fell back on the bed and stared at the ceiling, thinking about the stuff that Lila had lost. Her clothes, her jewelry, her letters, her pictures—

"Her pictures!" Jessica said out loud, sitting up quickly. Suddenly she knew *exactly* what would cheer Lila up—a photo album. Jessica would make a beautiful homemade photo album with all their pictures in it, from childhood to the present. It would be like a trip down memory lane.

Feeling energized, Jessica shoved some boxes out of the way and pushed through the mess on the floor. She had millions of pictures of Lila, and they dated back to childhood. Most of the photos were of their friends, but she even had pictures of Lila's family as well.

Standing on her tiptoes, Jessica reached for a stack of photo albums on the top shelf of her bookcase. She maneuvered her way back across the floor and dumped them on the bed. Then she knelt down and reached under her bed, pulling out a dusty yellow photo box.

Jessica sat down on the side of the bed and lifted off the lid of the box, dumping the carton upside down. A sea of old black-and-white photos scattered across the bedspread.

Sitting cross-legged, Jessica fished through the photos eagerly. She couldn't wait to give the photo album to Lila. Maybe she would see her best friend really smile for the first time since the fire.

"Well, it looks like Steven's a no-show again," Todd remarked on Thursday evening at the Sky Rink, an indoor ice-skating rink in downtown Sweet Valley.

Elizabeth and Todd were sitting on a bench outside the rental office, lacing up their skates while they waited for Steven. Steven had said he would join them at the rink after work.

Elizabeth leaned over and pulled her laces tight. "I'm sure he'll show up this time," she said. She propped her right foot up on the back of the blade and tied her laces in a double knot.

But inside she wasn't so sure. When Elizabeth had proposed the idea to Steven at breakfast, he had been decidedly unenthusiastic. He had only agreed to go after Mrs. Wakefield had pushed him.

Elizabeth sighed. Steven was so flaky lately that

he might not even remember their conversation. When she had confronted him at breakfast about not showing up last night for the movie, he had just stared at her. "What movie?" he asked.

And then he had refused to tell her where he had been the night before. "Oh, I was just out," he had said vaguely.

"Out where?" Elizabeth had demanded.

Steven had shrugged. "I really can't say," he finally said. "It had to do with business."

Steven's evasive behavior was only making her more concerned. Her brother wasn't acting like himself at all. He was closed and secretive, and he was working on the Fowler case day and night. *He's hiding in his work,* Elizabeth thought. *He probably misses Billie dreadfully.*

Todd stood up and took a few steps to test out his skates. "You ready?" he asked.

Elizabeth glanced at her watch. "Let's just wait a few minutes longer," she pleaded. "If Steven shows up and we're already out on the rink, he's going to feel like a third wheel."

Todd did a small turn on his skates. "You know, that's how *I'm* beginning to feel," he complained. "You're completely neglecting me. You don't have any interest in being out with me."

"Oh, Todd, that's ridiculous," Elizabeth scoffed.

"No, it's not," Todd insisted, crossing his arms over his chest. "You don't care about me anymore." He put a mock pout on his face.

"You know that's not true," Elizabeth responded.

"Then prove it to me," Todd said. He walked up to the bench and held out a hand.

"Oh, all right," Elizabeth agreed, taking his hand and letting him pull her up. "I guess a few turns around the rink can't hurt." Elizabeth tightened her ponytail and took a few preliminary steps.

They walked across the green turf and skated onto the smooth ice. It was dark and cool inside the oval arena. The place was almost deserted. A few couples were doing rotations hand in hand, and a girl in a skating skirt was spinning in the middle of the rink. Todd hooked his arm through Elizabeth's, and they skated together around the periphery.

Usually Elizabeth would find this the perfect environment for a date. They were practically all alone under the soft blue lights, and a romantic song was playing over the loudspeakers. But she couldn't get her brother out of her mind.

Elizabeth glanced over at the bench as they completed their rotation, but Steven wasn't there. "Where do you think he is?" she asked. "Do you think he's all alone in some dive, pining away for Billie?"

Todd groaned and skidded to a stop.

"Or maybe he's involved in something really dangerous for the D.A.'s office," she went on, her mind racing. "Maybe he's chasing after the arsonist."

Elizabeth frowned. She hadn't really thought about this possibility before, but it was very likely that Steven was in real danger. The Fowler Crest fire was serious business.

"Do you know what I think?" Todd asked, skating in small figure-eight patterns in the middle of the ice.

"What?" Elizabeth asked, drifting slowly backward. She hit the wall and grabbed onto the railing for support.

"I think Steven is a grown man who can take care of himself." Todd turned sharply, cutting into the ice and sending up a spray of fine powder.

Elizabeth bit her lip. "Yeah, I guess you're right."

Todd did a quick turn and skated up to her. "And I think we should take advantage of the fact that we're out alone together," he said softly.

Elizabeth looked down, feeling guilty for being such a bad date.

Suddenly Todd scooped her up in his arms and skated across the ice.

"To-odd!" Elizabeth yelped.

When they got to the middle of the rink, he turned in a rapid-fire circle, spinning her around wildly. "Todd! Let me down!" Elizabeth giggled, watching dizzily as the four walls of the skating rink zoomed past her.

"Of course," Todd said, slowing to a stop. He put her down gently and wrapped his arms around her, leaning in for a long, romantic kiss. After their spin on the ice, Todd's passionate kiss only made her feel giddier.

As Todd kissed her tenderly, Elizabeth could feel all her troubles melting away. His lips were soft and sweet on hers, and his arms were warm around her in the coolness of the rink. Elizabeth felt like they were in their own private universe.

Todd leaned back and smiled at her. "If you can't stop thinking about Steven, then I'm going to have to *make* you stop thinking about him," he said in a whisper.

Elizabeth leaned forward for another kiss. "I think it's working," she murmured.

Chapter 11

Steven sat alone in the den on Thursday evening, a sea of papers spread out on the table in front of him. He had stayed late at the D.A.'s office, running computer searches on George Fowler and his business associates. When the office had closed, he had crammed all the printouts in his briefcase and had brought them home with him.

Ever since his dinner with Lila the night before, Steven was infused with a new sense of urgency. If Lila was being followed at school, then she was in imminent danger. Steven was determined to prevent any new incident from taking place.

Steven leafed through the stack of papers on the coffee table and pulled out a long computer readout. It was a profile of arsonists in the southern California area. He'd read through it about a hundred times that day, trying to find a link to the Fowler case.

Steven held the report high in the air so the entire computer printout was visible. He had circled three possible suspects in red ink: Joe Harvey, a young underprivileged kid from Davis who had completely razed the prominent estate of the richest family in town; Mario Moretti, an insane guy who had tried to set city hall on fire a few years ago; and Dean James, a criminal expert who was responsible for a series of small infernos in the southern Los Angeles area.

The only problem was that all the suspects were out of commission. Joe was in a rehabilitation center in Berkeley, Mario Moretti was in a psychiatric ward, and Dean James was in jail. Steven had even called each institution to verify that none of the potential suspects were out on parole.

Sitting back, Steven scanned through the entire list again, wondering if he'd missed anyone. But all the other suspects were involved primarily in other kinds of crime—theft, murder, or embezzlement. They were criminals who had resorted to arson in order to cover up their felonies. The Fowler case was a pure act of arson. No other crime had been committed.

At least not yet, Steven thought, dropping the report on the table. Once again his thoughts returned to Lila, and he felt his chest tighten in anxiety. He wondered if she'd been followed again in school today. He and Lila had a meeting scheduled at Fowler Crest in an hour, but he longed to go over there now to make sure she was all right.

Steven shook his disturbing thoughts away. Worrying about Lila wasn't going to get him anywhere. The thing to do was get to the bottom of the case. He was determined to come up with something before he saw her tonight. If he had a lead, then maybe she could help him get to the source of the crime.

Since none of the arsonists seem credible, the fire must be connected directly to the Fowlers themselves, Steven thought, drumming his fingers on the arm of the chair. He flipped open his briefcase and pulled out a manila file marked Confidential. Laying the file open on his lap, he leafed quickly through the contents. He stopped at a list of George Fowler's business partners.

Steven whistled underneath his breath as he ran his index finger down the list. George Fowler had an impressive list of associates—the prince and princess of Monaco, the president of Lloyd's insurance of London, the chancellor of the German government. *No wonder Lila is used to mixing with the elite,* he thought. *Her father does business with royalty and heads of state.*

Steven's attention started to wane again. He remembered the joy in Lila's voice when she'd talked about oyster digging in the south of France and sailing on the Mediterranean Sea. He thought about the tiny curve to her mouth when she was amused and of the way her soft brown eyes lit up when she was excited.

Sighing deeply, Steven ran a hand through his hair. He had to keep his mind on his work. Sitting up straight, he forced himself to study the list again. But the words just blended together, and all he saw was Lila's image in his mind. Finally he gave up. *It's no use,* he realized. *I can't stop thinking about her.*

Steven clenched his jaw. He had to get ahold of himself. He was never going to crack the case if all he did was dream about Lila. But he found himself thinking about her constantly—when he was in his car driving to work, when he was sitting in his cubicle at the D.A.'s office, and when he was trying to work at home.

Two opposing images kept appearing before his eyes. In the first he imagined Lila staring wide-eyed in terror as hot flames swirled all around her. In the second he saw her setting the fire glee-fully—with the excitement he'd seen in her eyes when she talked about fishing for oysters in France or eating caviar in St. Petersburg.

Cold facts told him that the second image was the truth, especially after the news he'd gotten today. He'd placed a call to Lila's chauffeur, who claimed to know nothing about the can of gas found in Lila's car. In fact, he said he never carried spare gas. At the moment, Steven had to admit, everything pointed to Lila—the sulfur on her fingertips, the matches in the restaurant, the empty gas can in her car.

But his gut and heart told him Lila was innocent. She appeared to be genuinely frightened. And she seemed to be completely forthcoming and sincere.

But whichever possibility he saw, he couldn't get her out of his mind.

Devon climbed the stairs wearily on Thursday night to wash up before bed, completely out of sorts. Ever since the worker had confronted him that afternoon, he had been feeling disturbed. The man's drawling words reverberated in his mind. *Where I come from, it's called stealing.*

Devon frowned as he reached the second floor. Things had only gotten worse at dinner. His aunt wanted a new car, a station wagon with a hatchback. "Now that we're a family of five, the little Toyota just won't do," she had explained. And she had come up with an elaborate plan for another wing, complete with a studio and a study. "So you'll have a place to work in peace and quiet when you're in college," she had said.

"And for now we can use it as an office," his uncle had put in.

Devon headed down the hall, scowling. He felt as if he had started an avalanche. Now that the Wilsons had dipped their hands in the honey pot, they couldn't stop asking for more. Every day they wanted something new. And Devon didn't know what to do about it.

Devon flicked on the light in the bathroom and stared at his image in the mirror. His handsome face stared back at him, pale and implacable. His eyes were a cold, stony blue. *The eyes of somebody who doesn't trust anybody,* he thought. They were the eyes of somebody who was all alone in the world.

Devon turned on the faucet and splashed cold water on his face. Picking up a bar of soap, he scrubbed his face clean, trying to work off some of his aggression. Then he brushed his teeth viciously and rinsed out his mouth. Reaching for the hand towel, he dried off his face and drew a deep breath. *You're just being cynical,* he told himself. *You're being cynical and stingy. Money doesn't matter. People do.*

Devon repeated the words to himself as he passed by his aunt and uncle's bedroom. *Money doesn't matter. People do.* The door was open a crack, and he leaned in to say good night. But then he overheard his name spoken.

His heart beating, Devon flattened himself against the wall and listened to their conversation.

". . . and if we add in the price of the office," his aunt was saying, "the total comes to nearly a million dollars."

Devon felt his pulse speed up. They were

170

discussing the bills for all their new purchases.

His aunt shuffled some papers. "That's nearly a tenth of Devon's entire inheritance," she said.

"But we don't have it yet," his uncle said, sounding worried. "I met with the bank today, and they agreed to three separate loans." There was a pause. "I'm a little concerned about taking out so much debt."

"Oh, that's nothing," his aunt responded. "We'll have Devon's inheritance in our hands before the first interest payment is even due. We'll be able to pay off all the loans at once."

His uncle muttered something incomprehensible. Their voices got lower, and Devon couldn't make out any of the words. He heard the sounds of a chair scraping and footsteps across the floor. Holding his breath, Devon inched closer to the door. Once again their voices reached his ear.

" . . . rather high," his uncle was saying. "We probably should leave something for the boy."

"Oh, he won't even miss a million," his aunt scoffed. "Besides, what does he need it for? Ohio State University is practically free. And he'll come into the rest of the money when he's twenty-one." There was a pause, and then she said, "That's only a couple of years away." Her voice got lower. "Maybe we can get that house on the lake we've always talked about."

The two of them laughed softly together.

Devon closed his eyes tightly, feeling like he'd

been physically struck. He had known it was too good to be true. He knew that they didn't really care about him. They just wanted to use him, like everybody else. Devon felt his heart hardening, like it had so often before.

Well, he decided as he headed down the hall, *there's only one thing left to do.* He'd make sure they had everything they wanted. And they'd get exactly what they deserved.

Lila paced along the red clay tiles of the patio on Thursday night, waiting impatiently for Steven to come over. She hadn't been able to sit still all evening. She had the eerie feeling that somebody was out to get her. Once again she had felt a presence behind her all day in school, and she was sure that somebody had followed her home. Now she was entirely spooked.

Lila heard the sound of a door creaking inside the house and jumped. She stood perfectly still and waited. Sure enough, the noise repeated itself. Her heart began to sound a drumroll in her chest. Lila crept to the back door and slipped inside the den. Standing flat against the wall, she held her breath and listened. She couldn't hear anything, but she had the uncanny sensation that she wasn't alone.

Lila tiptoed through the den to the living room, which was barren and dusty. The rooms were all clean and empty now. None of the ruined furniture remained. The walls had been repainted, and new floorboards had been laid. The doors and windows had been replaced as well. Now the house seemed even more foreign than ever.

Sticking close to the walls, Lila crept around the living room to the front hall. She thought she heard the quiet *whish* of clothing. Her blood roaring in her ears, she glanced around the corner. A shadow appeared on the wall and disappeared. Her eyes wide with fear, Lila peeked into the foyer. Nobody was there. And the front door was firmly shut.

Lila wrapped her arms around herself, shaking violently. *Am I going crazy?* she wondered. *Am I seeing things?*

Feeling terrified, Lila turned and fled. She ran through the empty rooms as fast as she could and pushed open the back door. Her heart rate began to slow down as she hurried across the lawn. *Maybe my friends were right,* she thought. *Maybe I shouldn't be staying alone in the house with an arsonist on the loose.*

But then her pride returned to her. It was bad enough that somebody had dared to invade her privacy and burn down her house. She refused to be chased out of her home. She refused to be scared away.

Lila pushed open the door to the pool house and sat down on the edge of the cot. She wrapped her arms around her body, still trembling slightly. *Steven will be here any minute now,* she reassured herself. *He'll take all my fears away.*

Thank goodness she had someone to help her through all this. She remembered Steven's comforting words from the night before. *I'm with you,* he had said. *I won't let anything happen to you.* With Steven to come by and visit, even living in the pool house didn't seem so bad. It had a great view, and it was small and cozy.

Just then Lila heard a low knock on the door. Her heart leapt into her throat, and for a moment she was paralyzed with fear. But then a familiar male voice spoke up. "Lila?" he called. "It's me, Steven."

Lila let out a shuddering breath, feeling like her prayers had been answered. She hurried to the door and flung it open. Steven stood in the entranceway, a serious expression on his handsome face.

"Steven!" Lila exclaimed. "I'm so glad to see you!"

Steven nodded and didn't respond, obviously all business. He walked across the floor and took a seat at the table. "There appears to be a new piece of evidence," he said.

"There is?" Lila said eagerly, feeling her hopes soar. She knew Steven would find the person who set the fire. Maybe this nightmare had an end in sight after all.

But Steven looked grim. "Unfortunately the evidence points to you," he said. "Again."

Steven pulled something out of his pocket and

174

held it up. Lila frowned as she recognized it. It was a pair of monogrammed Italian gloves that her father had given her for her birthday. Her initials were engraved on the cuffs. She took the soft, brown leather gloves from him and studied them. They seemed to be soaked in gas.

"But . . . but these are mine," Lila murmured, confused.

"I know," Steven responded. "And this time I'm the one who found them. They were lying in front of the bushes outside the house." Steven shook his head. "I don't know how I missed them before."

Lila's high spirits evaporated into shock. So somebody really *had* been in the house earlier. And now their motives were clear—they were trying to frame her. It looked like Steven had walked right into the trap. Lila sat down in a chair across from him. "Steven, please say you don't think I started the fire," she implored.

Steven was silent. He just stared at the floor, his face set.

"Steven, I had *nothing* to do with this. You've *got* to believe me," Lila said, her hand fluttering nervously in the air. "I heard somebody in the house earlier, but when I got there, they were already gone. Obviously I'm being set up."

Steven didn't look convinced. "You have to say that, don't you?"

Lila stood up, indignant. She was shocked that Steven was turning on her like this. She couldn't believe he actually thought she was capable of setting her own house on fire. Lila stared at him angrily. "Why would I leave 'evidence' where I knew you'd find it?" she demanded hotly, her hands on her hips.

Steven shrugged, unmoved. "Maybe you can tell me that," he said softly.

Tears sprang to Lila's eyes. She felt like the rug was being pulled out from under her. Suddenly her sole support was gone. Steven seemed like a total stranger. Now she was all alone in the world, and she was in danger. Terrible danger. Lila sank down on the cot in despair. "Someone's out to get me," she said in a shaking voice. "You can see that, can't you?"

Steven's expression softened, and the tender look returned to his eyes. "Yes, I can," he said softly. He stood up and took a seat next to her on the cot.

"I'm scared, Steven," Lila said in a tiny voice.

"I know," Steven said, wrapping his arms around her. Lila rested her head on his broad chest, and he rubbed a comforting hand on her back. "Shhh," he whispered into her ear. "It's going to be OK."

Lila's fears faded away in his strong arms. Steven did care about her after all. He couldn't hold her like this if he thought she was guilty.

Chapter 12

Steven arrived at work on Friday in a funk. It was getting harder and harder for him to deny the evidence. The matches in Lila's pocket, the empty gas can in her car, the gas-soaked gloves with her initials on them . . . The cold, hard facts were staring him in the face, and he couldn't ignore them any longer.

Steven dropped his briefcase on the floor by his desk and headed straight for the coffee machine. He had barely slept at all the night before. The case had kept him awake for hours as he turned the evidence over and over in his mind. But he couldn't seem to make heads or tails out of any of it.

"You look like you could use a cup of high-test," James Harrison remarked, joining him at the coffee machine with a white mug in his hand. James was a young attorney with a relaxed attitude and a casual style of dressing. But supposedly he was a ruthless prosecutor who never left a case unsolved.

Steven nodded ruefully. "I could use about five cups," he said, reaching for an insulated paper cup from the stack on the table.

James picked up the coffeepot and filled his mug. "So, are you making progress on the Fowler case?" he asked.

Steven shrugged. "I guess so," he said. James handed him the coffeepot, and Steven poured himself a cup.

"Well, Joe says you're doing a great job," James said, dropping a sugar cube into his coffee. "Don't get discouraged."

"Thanks, James," Steven said, walking back to his cubicle.

Steven shook his head as he sat down at his desk. Every time he was with Lila, she managed to convince him she was innocent. Her wide eyes and her sweet smile were irresistible. When she stared at him with her imploring gaze, all his suspicions disappeared into thin air. But as soon as he left her his reason returned to him with a vengeance.

Why would she do it? he asked himself for the twentieth time. The question was tormenting him. Steven opened his briefcase and took out his files, setting them on his desk. Taking a gulp of black coffee, he reached for the mail in his in box.

Steven casually flipped through the stack of flyers and notices. It all looked unimportant. There was a memo announcing an office picnic, a notice about a new espresso machine, and an invitation to some lawyers' banquet. The rest just looked like junk mail. Steven picked up the entire stack and dumped it in the trash.

Then he noticed something in the bottom of his in box. Steven lifted it out, glancing at it with curiosity. It was a copy of a Web page, and it detailed the profile of an arsonist. Steven turned it over, but there was no note attached to it. He had no idea who'd sent it.

Steven read through the profile with growing alarm.

An arsonist
    -is crying out for help and attention
    -needs affection, nurturing, and security
    -needs excitement
    -feels tension or emotional arousal before the act
    -is fascinated by fire paraphernalia

Steven sat back in his chair, his mind clicking. He went through the items one by one to see if they applied to Lila. The first point was obvious. Lila could easily have been trying to get her parents' attention. When she had finally gotten her mother back, Grace had immediately gallivanted off on a second honeymoon with Lila's father. And now her parents had left her alone again, with no hope of contacting them. Clearly Lila must feel neglected.

Steven himself could vouch for the second category.

Every time he was with her, Lila turned to him for nurturing and emotional support. She had repeatedly thanked him for being there for her during this difficult time. And she seemed happiest when she was in his arms. He thought of the way she had snuggled up to him last night in the pool house.

Does Lila need excitement? Steven asked himself. The answer was clearly affirmative. She was used to going on exotic vacations and mixing with royalty. Steven didn't know when he'd met a girl with such a fearless quality and an adventurous spirit. Steven took a sip of coffee, his eyes narrowed in thought. Maybe life in Sweet Valley had gotten too boring for her so she'd decided to drum up some excitement.

Steven set down his cup and turned to the next item—experiences tension before the act. Well, that wasn't hard to imagine. Lila had just broken up with her old boyfriend and had been in an emotionally distraught state. In fact, she was deliberately burning his love letters. The fire could clearly have provoked a sort of emotional release.

Finally Steven got to the last item: fascinated by fire paraphernalia. He frowned as he realized that this item was right on the mark too. He thought of how Lila had stared dreamily into the flickering candlelight at dinner on Wednesday night and how she had pocketed a book of matches on her way out.

Steven set down the page, his heart sinking. Lila met every single criterion from the Web page.

She matched the portrait of an arsonist exactly. Steven crumpled his paper cup and threw it in the trash, feeling discouraged.

Only one question remained. Where did the Web page come from? Steven stood up and headed to his boss's office. It would make sense that the D.A. would have sent it to him. After all, he had been convinced from the start that Lila was guilty. And Mr. Garrison had a tendency to send him unsigned memos.

Steven knocked lightly on his boss's door.

"Come in!" he responded, his voice harsh.

Mr. Garrison was in a meeting with two town prosecutors. They were sitting around the small round table by the window, a mountain of legal memos and briefs in front of them.

"Oh, excuse me," Steven said. "It wasn't important."

But the D.A. waved him in. "What's on your mind?" he asked, walking over to the door.

Steven quickly showed him the Web page. "I was wondering if you'd sent this to me," he explained.

Mr. Garrison squinted at the computer printout. "No," he said slowly. "I've never seen it before." He took the page from Steven's hand and glanced through it. "Looks interesting, though."

"OK, thanks," Steven said, backing out the door.

"Oh, and Steven," Mr. Garrison said. "Stop by this afternoon."

"Sure," Steven agreed.

"And bring the Web page with you," his boss

added. Then he turned abruptly back to his meeting.

Steven was perplexed. If Mr. Garrison hadn't sent him the Web page, then one of the attorneys must have dropped it in his box. But it was surprising that they hadn't left a note. Steven stopped by James Harrison's cubicle. He was hunched over his desk, his face buried in a thick legal book.

"Sorry to interrupt you," Steven said. "I was wondering if you'd dropped this profile in my box."

James looked up from his book. "What profile?" he asked.

Steven handed him the page.

James pushed his thin black glasses up on his nose and studied it. "Nope, can't say I did."

"OK, thanks," Steven said, heading for the next cubicle.

Steven spent the next fifteen minutes asking around the office, but nobody had any idea where the Web page came from. Finally he headed to the receptionist's desk. Since nobody in the office was responsible for the page, it must have come from the outside.

Steven stepped up to the front desk to talk to Adele, the receptionist. He'd developed a lot of respect for her in the last few days. She had decided to go to law school at the age of forty and was in her last year. She was working at the D.A.'s office part-time in order to help support her children. At the moment she was hitting the phone lines and sending a fax at the same time.

"Do you know where this came from?" Steven

asked when she had gotten off the phone. He laid the Web page down on the desk.

Adele looked at it carefully, but then she shook her head. "No, it didn't go through me."

"But it doesn't make any sense," Steven said, picking up the printout and folding it in half. "It couldn't have just appeared out of thin air."

"Oh, well, one of the detectives probably dropped it off," Adele said with a shrug.

Steven headed back to his cubicle, his spirits low. Wherever the Web page had come from, he wished he'd never seen it.

Devon walked down the steps to the living room on Friday evening, where the entire family was gathered after dinner. Their voices were raised in anger, and they were talking so loudly that Devon had been able to hear them all the way upstairs. Apparently they were having an all-out war, fighting over the pieces of their new pie.

Devon hesitated in the hall, listening to their bickering.

"A Porsche! That's ridiculous!" Aunt Peggy scoffed. "If we're going to get a new car, we're going to get the best. I won't settle for anything less than a Cadillac."

"A Cadillac!" Ross put in. "That's so stuffy. Can't we get a sports car?"

"Now, Ross, you shouldn't complain," Uncle Mark interjected. "You just got a brand-new motorbike."

"It's not fair!" Allan chimed in. "Ross got a cool motorbike and all I got was a stupid old bicycle."

"It's not a stupid old bicycle," Ross retorted. "It's the brand-new mountain bike that you said you wanted."

"Well, it already has a dent in it," Allan pouted.

"Boys, please," Aunt Peggy said. "Your father and I are having a discussion."

Ross mumbled something that Devon couldn't hear, and the boys quieted down.

"Now, Mark, I wanted to discuss my sitting room with you," Aunt Peggy said. "As soon as the construction is finished I'm going to hire a pair of interior designers to do the decorating. I thought we could do it up in an Early American style." She paused. "And we might as well redecorate the kitchen while we're at it."

"Your sitting room?" Uncle Mark exploded. "I thought that was going to be my study!"

"No, silly," Aunt Peggy said. "You'll get your office when we build the next wing."

Devon laughed bitterly to himself. *Her* sitting room was supposed to be *his* new bedroom. So he would feel at home. Just like one of the family. And Uncle Mark's office was supposed to be his study.

It's all my fault, Devon thought, leaning against the wall outside the room. He himself had wrought all this by feeding their greedy fantasies. Devon sighed quietly. He should have put his foot down from the start. *Well,* he thought, *it will all be over soon enough.*

184

Taking a deep breath, Devon entered the room. The whole family fell silent, staring at him with guilty expressions on their faces.

"Oh, hi, Devon!" Aunt Peggy exclaimed, giving him a big, fake smile.

"Hi," Devon muttered, staring at his feet.

Suddenly everybody went back to what they had been doing. Aunt Peggy sat down in the armchair and resumed her sewing; Uncle Mark sat down on the couch and picked up the newspaper; the kids flopped down on the rug and started dealing cards.

Devon shifted from one foot to the other, feeling suddenly nervous. It was time to drop the bomb. Even though he knew what the outcome would be, he couldn't help holding on to a tiny thread of hope that he had a family here. He couldn't help wishing that they'd say it didn't matter, that he was family, that they loved him with or without his money.

Devon took a deep breath. "I have some news," he announced.

They all looked at him expectantly.

"I just spoke to my family lawyer on the phone," Devon said. "It turns out that my parents' estate is bankrupt."

The entire family was silent. Devon held his breath, hoping beyond hope that they would surprise him.

Suddenly tension split the air.

"What?" Aunt Peggy exclaimed.

"Bankrupt!" Uncle Mark repeated.

"There's no money?" Ross asked.

The three of them stared him down, like hunters after their prey.

"I'm really sorry," Devon said, taking a step back.

"But . . . but what do you mean—bankrupt?" Aunt Peggy spluttered, jumping up. "What in the world are you talking about?"

"Well, apparently my father had a lot of business debts," Devon said slowly. "The estate had to claim bankruptcy to cover them."

"Bankruptcy!" Aunt Peggy exclaimed. "Why . . . why, that's ludicrous! That's absolutely outrageous!" She turned to Devon, her eyes shooting ice blue sparks. "Why didn't you tell us?"

"I'm sorry," Devon said again. "I just found out about it today."

"There's no money at all?" Uncle Mark asked.

Devon shook his head. "None."

"We're ruined," Uncle Mark said, putting his hands to his head in despair.

"How dare you!" Aunt Peggy yelled, coming at Devon. "We've taken out three loans! The work is already started on the house! It's too late to back out now!"

Devon backed up quickly, feeling his heart constrict in his chest. Sweet Aunt Peggy was having a complete personality transformation. In the space of a minute she had gone from kind and gentle to almost maniacal. Her eyes were bulging in rage, and angry blue veins popped out on the sides of her neck.

But Aunt Peggy shook him off. "Devon, this is all your fault!" she screamed hysterically, waving her index finger in the air. "You got us into this; now you get us out of it!"

"Does this mean I don't get my motorbike?" Allan asked.

"It means we don't get *anything*," Ross pouted.

"I guess you'll be wanting me to move on now," Devon said quietly.

"You ready for our conference?" Elizabeth said on Friday evening, crossing through the bathroom that connected the twins' bedrooms. The girls had decided to hold a meeting to discuss their plan to cheer up Lila and Steven. Jessica's door was shut, and Elizabeth knocked softly.

"Ready!" Jessica called out.

Elizabeth opened the door, and her mouth dropped open. Jessica's room was literally covered with clothing. Pants and T-shirts were piled up knee-high on the floor, and skirts and dresses were draped over every available surface. Empty boxes were stacked up in the corner, and open shopping bags were scattered all over the floor.

"I have never seen so many clothes in my whole life!" Elizabeth exclaimed, pushing open the door with an effort and stepping gingerly into the room.

"Yeah, isn't it great?" Jessica asked. She was sitting in the middle of the floor between two piles of clothes, folding up some T-shirts.

"I guess so," Elizabeth said, eyeing the mountains of clothing dubiously. "Lila certainly has a whole new wardrobe here."

"Do you want to see what we bought?" Jessica offered. She pushed aside some shoes and laid the folded-up T-shirts in a neat stack on the floor.

"Sure," Elizabeth responded, carefully making her way through the piles of clothing. A wall of coats blocked the bed, and she climbed over them. Shoving some shopping bags onto the floor, she settled on the bed with her back against the wall. "OK, bring it on."

Jessica picked through some clothes on the floor and pulled out a short, hip-hugging tangerine-colored skirt and a pale blue silk T-shirt. She threw off her jeans and T-shirt, adding them to one of the piles on the floor. Then she carefully put on the outfit.

"Hey, that's great!" Elizabeth said admiringly when Jessica was dressed. The ensemble suited Jessica perfectly. The skirt hung elegantly at the hip, and the T-shirt brought out the color of her ocean blue eyes. "I like how the skirt falls."

"That's why we got it," Jessica said, walking forward and swishing her hips like a model.

"Is the T-shirt silk?" Elizabeth asked, squinting from the bed.

"Yeah, it's raw silk," Jessica said. "It's really soft."

She sashayed toward the bed to show her but tripped over the coats, landing belly first on the bed.

"Yow!" Jessica exclaimed, flipping over onto her back.

"Careful!" Elizabeth cautioned, shaking her head. "You know, I think you're the only person in this world who can make shopping dangerous." She leaned forward to feel the silky material of the T-shirt.

Jessica grinned. "Very few people understand the perils of the profession," she said, sliding off the bed. She grabbed a short, fitted black raincoat from her chair and slipped it on. "What do you think of this?"

The raincoat was beautiful. It was made of a sleek, rubbery material that was surprisingly elegant. The form suited Jessica as well. It tapered in at the waist and flared out at the hips, highlighting Jessica's figure. Elizabeth whistled under her breath. "Ve-ry chic," she said.

"These are all the rage in Paris," Jessica said. She tried to do a turn but got tangled up in a sweater and collapsed on the floor. "Humph," she pouted.

"It's funny how Lila's purchases are all perfect on you," Elizabeth remarked.

"That's because the shopping spree has totally bombed with Lila," Jessica said with a sigh, falling back on a stack of sweaters in an exaggerated gesture of despair. "I'm the one doing all the work."

"Well, I haven't done much to cheer up Steven either," Elizabeth admitted. "He keeps standing me and Todd up." She sighed. "Of course, we have ended up having some nice dates."

189

"Liz, believe me, I think it's much better for Steven that he wasn't there to witness your happiness," Jessica said, sitting up.

"Well, what are we going to do now?" Elizabeth asked. "Clearly my plan is a total failure."

Jessica stood and stepped carefully through the clothing. "Well, I came up with a counterplan last night," she said. She picked up a few of the coats and flung them across the room. Then she sat down on the side of the bed, her blue-green eyes sparkling.

"You did?" Elizabeth asked.

Jessica nodded. "I'm making Lila a photo album. I decided to give her something that would have some meaning for her."

"That's a great idea!" Elizabeth enthused.

Jessica leaned over and picked up a bound book from the floor. "Well, I'm not done yet, but this is what I have so far." She handed her creation to Elizabeth.

Elizabeth placed the half-finished book on her lap. Jessica had done a beautiful job. She had bound together delicate pieces of gold paper with thick black tape, and the whole book closed with a silver clasp. Elizabeth turned to the first page. An array of black-and-white baby shots of Jessica and Lila was displayed. On the next page there were pictures of the two of them as kids, playing in a sandbox. "You're starting from childhood!" Elizabeth exclaimed.

Jessica nodded excitedly. "Look at this shot,"

she said, carefully turning to the next page. It featured an enlarged close-up of Jessica and Lila having a snowball fight. Jessica was wearing a red snowsuit, and Lila was in a long-sleeve woolen dress.

Elizabeth shook her head, impressed. "Jessica, this is really fantastic."

"Well, it's not done yet," Jessica said, taking the album from her hands. "But I think she's going to like it."

Suddenly Elizabeth was struck with an idea. "Why don't I do the same thing for Steven?" she said, thinking out loud. "I could make a romantic memory book of Steven and Billie."

Jessica stared at her in shock. "Are you insane?" she asked incredulously. "That would be cruel."

"Yeah, of course it would," Elizabeth said, wondering what she had been thinking. Obviously pictures of Billie wouldn't cheer Steven up. They would just depress him further. Elizabeth reached for a throw pillow and tucked it behind her back, feeling discouraged. "But I just don't know what to do about Steven," she said. "We've got to come up with a new idea to cheer him up."

"Hmmm," Jessica said. "That's a tall order." She leaned over and placed the photo album carefully at the head of her bed. "Steven's been a comatose case lately."

"What if we invited Billie here for the weekend?" Elizabeth suggested.

Jessica shook her head. "She would say no."

"Well, then, what if we arranged for them to meet without telling them?" Elizabeth proposed.

But Jessica shook her head again. "Liz, Steven and Billie are *history*. It's time for him to move on." She drummed her fingers on the side of the bed. "But you've given me an idea. What if we set Steven up on a blind date?"

Elizabeth frowned. "Absolutely not!" she said. "I don't want to be responsible for driving Steven and Billie any further apart." Elizabeth heaved a sigh. She couldn't imagine that Steven could ever be happy without Billie in his life, but she didn't know how to get them back together. "Well, I can't think of anything else," she said finally.

"I'm sure we'll come up with something," Jessica reassured her. She wriggled out of the raincoat and threw it on a chair. "For the moment I'll show you the rest of the loot. If you want, I could put on a fashion show."

"That sounds like fun," Elizabeth agreed, glad to take a break from worrying about Steven. "Why don't we grab some chips and salsa and make a night of it?"

Chapter 13

"Lila, you have *got* to come clean!" Steven insisted on Friday evening in the Wakefield kitchen. Lila had stopped by to see him unexpectedly, and Steven had cracked at the sight of her. She had barely had time to take off her coat before he had launched into an interrogation.

"But Steven, I have nothing to come clean *about*," Lila responded, spreading her hands out wide in a gesture of innocence. She took a seat on one of the stools at the counter. Steven could see her looking at him like he was crazy while he roamed the kitchen floor, but he didn't care. He couldn't take it anymore. He had to get to the bottom of this once and for all.

Steven walked up to the counter and stood directly in front of her. "Lila, please, just tell me the truth," he begged her. "If you were lonely, if you needed attention, if you were searching for affection, you *have* to tell me."

Steven could see Lila's jaw clench. "Yes, I was lonely, and yes, I wanted attention!" Lila confessed, holding her chin high. "There, are you satisfied?" She turned away from him angrily.

Steven held his breath, waiting for her to continue.

Lila whirled around, tears streaking down her cheeks. "But that's all I have to confess! I have nothing else to say!" Her hands were balled into fists at her sides.

Steven grabbed hold of her hands gently, trying to make her calm down. "If you had anything to do with that fire, you've got to tell me," he implored.

"I told you; I didn't do it," Lila said. Her voice was low and controlled. "I didn't have anything to do with it."

Steven sighed and ran a hand through his disheveled hair. "Lila, listen, I'm on your side," he said. "I want to help you. But I can't help you if I don't know the truth."

Lila's jaw tightened visibly. "I *have* told you the truth," she said, speaking through clenched teeth.

Steven sank down in a chair at the kitchen table, feeling defeated. "Lila, don't you understand? If you were the one who set the fire, the D.A.'s office is going to find out eventually. They're professionals." He dropped his head in his hands. "But if you let me know, I can help you. We can work this out together."

Lila looked like she was about to explode. She stood up and paced across the room. "Isn't it crystal clear that I'm being set up?" she asked, the frustration plain in her voice. "How much more evidence do you need?" She ticked off the items on her fingers as she spoke. "I almost die in a fire, I'm shadowed at school, and somebody plants a gas can in my car and gas-soaked gloves in my yard."

Lila walked back across the room. "If you want to find the right person, you should find out who's planting the evidence," she said. Lila stared straight at him, her eyes narrowed in fury. "For an intern at the D.A.'s office you're not very astute. Maybe you should go after the culprit instead of the victim."

Steven recoiled at Lila's sharp words. Her biting tone hit him like a ton of bricks. And once again he didn't know if he should believe her. Steven stared at her, torn. She sounded so sincere, and she looked so angry.

Lila grabbed her jacket from the chair and pulled it on. "If you don't trust me, we have nothing else to say to each other," she said quietly. Then she turned and headed for the door, holding her head high.

"Lila!" Steven called out, jumping up. "Please don't go!"

"Why shouldn't I?" she asked, turning around. Her face was flushed, and her hair was wild. She looked beautiful and tormented.

Steven hesitated at the sight of her. Despite her defiant gaze he could see the pain in her eyes. He felt like his heart was breaking in two. "I do trust you," he said softly.

Lila turned and walked back to him. "Look me in

the eyes and say you believe me," she commanded.

Steven stared deep into her eyes, feeling himself irresistibly drawn to her. She wrapped her arms around his neck and gazed back at him, her luminous brown eyes sparkling with unshed tears. Steven finally gave in to the longing that had been building up inside him all week. With a low groan he captured her lips with his.

Devon was back on his bike, ready to make another exit. He was alone again in the dark of night, with nothing to accompany him but the stars.

Devon took one last look at the cheery redbrick house with the well-kept front lawn and the white picket fence. He remembered the warm greeting he had received when he'd arrived on Sunday morning. He thought of the love he'd imagined seeing on his aunt and uncle's faces when they had welcomed him into their home.

And then he thought of the way he was leaving them. They hadn't even bothered to accompany him to the door. After the scene in the living room his aunt had practically thrown him out of the house. Devon had packed up his few belongings and had quietly let himself out the back door.

A gust of cool night air whipped through the trees, and Devon pulled his brown leather jacket tightly around him. He slowly revved the engine, his heart heavy.

How did everything go so wrong? he wondered.

He was leaving behind a family on the verge of destruction. Their lives were in hock, and their name was about to be sullied in town due to broken promises. Devon shrugged and adjusted his helmet. It was their own doing. They had gotten exactly what they deserved.

But Devon was scarred as well. He had been disappointed again. Now he had even less hope than before. Now he had even less faith in people. And it had been his mistake. He had confused normal and average with loving and kind.

Devon vowed not to make the same mistake again. His next stop was the home of his uncle Pete in Las Vegas. Uncle Pete was the black sheep of the family. Maybe not so perfect would turn out to be better than more than perfect, he thought.

Devon sat back in his seat. *Isn't there anyone out there who's kind and genuine and caring?* he wondered in despair. He searched for the North Star to guide him on his way. But the sky was pitch-black, and the star was nowhere to be seen.

Feeling as if he was all alone in the world, Devon revved the engine and headed off into the night.

"Do you think we should ask Steven if he wants to join us?" Elizabeth suggested as she and Jessica headed downstairs to fix their snack.

"Li-iz!" Jessica groaned. "That plan is out, remember?"

Elizabeth sighed and pushed a loose strand of

hair out of her eyes. "Yeah, that's right."

"Don't worry," Jessica said reassuringly. "We'll come up with something tonight. I guarantee it."

"I hope so," Elizabeth said, sounding unconvinced.

When they reached the foyer, Elizabeth paused. "I think I left a glass in the living room earlier," she said. "I'll be with you in a sec."

Jessica nodded and headed to the kitchen, her spirits high. Her parents were out for the evening, and she and Elizabeth had the house to themselves. For once she was in the mood to spend an evening at home with her sister. After her exhausting week at the mall, there was nothing she would rather do than munch on some chips and hot salsa and put on a fashion show. It was a relief to stop worrying about Lila and Steven for a few hours.

Jessica turned the corner and pushed open the kitchen door. Then she gasped and stopped in her tracks.

Steven and Lila were wrapped up in a heated embrace in the middle of the kitchen. Steven's arms were wrapped around Lila's waist, and her hands were tangled in his hair. They were kissing so passionately that they didn't even notice they had company.

Jessica recoiled in disgust. This definitely wasn't what she had meant when she said Steven should date other girls. She had been talking about college freshmen, not high-school girls, not *Lila*.

Jessica shook her head. Her brother and her best friend? It was too gross to contemplate.

But there they were, right in front of her eyes.

Just then Elizabeth appeared at her side. "What's wrong?" she asked.

But Jessica couldn't speak. She just waved a hand into the kitchen.

Elizabeth peeked her head through the doorway and then she backed out quickly, grabbing onto Jessica's arm for support. Her mouth was open, and her eyes were wide with shock.

"Steven and Lila?" Elizabeth asked, her face incredulous.

Jessica nodded, feeling as if she were seeing a carbon copy of herself. She knew the look of disgust in her twin's eyes mirrored her own.

Will Steven find a way to clear Lila's name and save their burning passion, or will his new flame be locked away for good? With his own sisters scheming to break up his romance, Steven could be headed for a major meltdown. Don't miss a moment of the red-hot action in Sweet Valley High #136, **Too Hot to Handle,** *the second book in this explosive three-part miniseries.*

Bantam Books in the Sweet Valley High series
Ask your bookseller for the books you have missed

SIGN UP FOR THE
SWEET VALLEY HIGH®
FAN CLUB!

Hey, girls! Get all the gossip on Sweet
Valley High's® most popular teenagers
when you join our fantastic Fan Club!
As a member, you'll get all of this really
cool stuff:

- Membership Card with your own
  personal Fan Club ID number
- A Sweet Valley High® Secret
  Treasure Box
- Sweet Valley High® Stationery
- Official Fan Club Pencil (for secret
  note writing!)
- Three Bookmarks
- A "Members Only" Door Hanger
- Two Skeins of J. & P. Coats® Embroidery
  Floss with flower barrette instruction
  leaflet
- Two editions of *The Oracle* newsletter
- Plus exclusive Sweet Valley High®
  product offers, special savings,
  contests, and much more!

Be the first to find out what Jessica & Elizabeth Wakefield are up to by joining the
Sweet Valley High® Fan Club for the one-year membership fee of only $6.25 each
for U.S. residents, $8.25 for Canadian residents (U.S. currency). Includes shipping
& handling.

Send a check or money order (do not send cash) made payable to "Sweet Valley
High® Fan Club" along with this form to:

SWEET VALLEY HIGH® FAN CLUB, BOX 3919-B, SCHAUMBURG, IL 60168-3919

NAME_____
            (Please print clearly)

ADDRESS_____

CITY_____ STATE _____ ZIP_____
                                                              (Required)

AGE_____ BIRTHDAY_____ /_____ /_____

Offer good while supplies last. Allow 6-8 weeks after check clearance for delivery. Addresses without ZIP
codes cannot be honored. Offer good in USA & Canada only. Void where prohibited by law.
©1993 by Francine Pascal   LCI-1383-123